# BUCKHEAD
# DEAD

Book One in the SKYE SOUTHERLAND Cozy Mystery Series

MARTINIQUE

# DEBORAH MALONE

A LAMP POST BOOK

BUCKHEAD DEAD
*By Deborah Malone*

ISBN 13: 978-1-60039-233-7
ebook ISBN: 978-1-60039-740-0

Copy Edit / Back Cover Copy: Melissa Williams Netherton

Scripture quotations are from the Holy Bible, English Standard Version, copyright © 2001, 2007 by Crossway Bibles, a division of Good News Publishers. Used by permission. All rights reserved.

www.lamppostpubs.com

# BUCKHEAD
# DEAD

Book One in the SKYE SOUTHERLAND Cozy Mystery Series

*Deborah Malone*

## BY DEBORAH MALONE

Do not judge by appearances,
but judge with right judgment.

John 7:24 (ESV)

# ACKNOWLEDGEMENTS

I would like to thank the City of Rome Police Department for their help with police procedure.

I want to thank Beverly Nault, who has edited all my books. She has the ability to get into my characters heads and keep them on the straight and narrow path, as they have a tendency to stray at times. Looking forward to working together on more books in the future.

Thank you Debra Collins for your friendship and encouragement. Dawn Hampton, thank you for your invaluable help breathing life into my characters. Zack Waters, thanks for always encouraging me and giving me that push to submit my first manuscript.

# Dedication

First and foremost, I want to dedicate *Buckhead Dead* to my beautiful daughters, Leah and Niki. Next, to all those who have read my books, sent me encouraging emails, or asked, "When's the next book coming out?" You keep me writing.

Last but not least, a special dedication to Book Ends book club in Dahlonega, Georgia who took me under their wing and made me a part of their family.

# BUCKHEAD DEAD

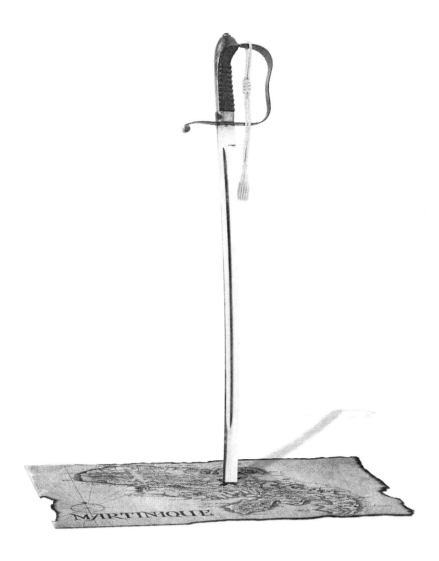

# CHAPTER ONE

"You're not serious? We were at her house just last night." I couldn't believe Sylvia had died. I pushed my glasses a little higher. Having just turned fifty, I deemed seeing clearly, more important than my vanity. I now considered wearing glasses a fashion statement.

"I'm serious as a dog after a bone, Skye. Stabbed right through the heart," Honey said.

Honey's high-pitched voice shot though the phone and pulled me back to earth. "Skye! I said I thought the Buckhead Diva would live forever. I don't think anybody really knew her age. She sure wouldn't tell." Honey should know because I'd heard her ask Sylvia Landmark her age on more than one occasion – with no success. If I guessed her age, I'd say about twenty years older than me. Even so, I considered seventy-five too young to die in my book.

My mind conjured images of the decorating job we'd just finished for Sylvia. I do believe I outdid myself. I've been the owner of Stylish Décor for over ten years now, and Honey Truelove, my best friend and assistant, has helped me nine of those years.

I wondered what my husband, Mitch, would have to say about the turn of events. He spends a great deal of time traveling the world to find unique and distinctive pieces for his antique shop. Due to arrive home today from a trip to Europe, I looked forward to seeing him.

*1*

"Skye! Did you hear me?"

"Uh, yeah, I did Honey." I thought about the work we did for Sylvia. She was quite alive last night at the party. Who would've imagined she'd die during the night? Well, she had to be close to eighty; one can't be expected to live forever. "Did you say she had a heart attack?"

"Good grief, sometimes I wonder if you don't tune me out. I said probably murdered." I pictured Honey with her customary hand on her hip and signature Merle Norman Romance Red lipstick pout.

I agreed. I did tune her out at times; in my defense I cherished my sanity. Did she ever love to talk. But this is one time I didn't mind she had the scoop on Sylvia. "Murdered? Who in the world would want to murder an old woman? I admit she was snooty and condescending at times, but is that reason enough to murder a person?" My glasses slid down again. *I need to get these things adjusted.*

"Hold on just a minute, Skye, I need to feed Sam." I heard her rummaging around in the kitchen. Sam is short for Samantha. With Honey's grown children now on their own, she treated Sam like a child. I could make out her words over the kibble filling the Yorkie's bowl. "You have to admit she was on a roll last night at the party. I don't think anyone escaped her blows. Except us, of course."

I agreed she took jabs at more than one person. "That's because we were on her good side since we've just finished redecorating her house. She especially loved the Elizabethan sleigh bed." She raved on and on about our artistic skills and how much better her house looked. She planned the party to show off her newly acquired antiques. She didn't mind rubbing a few people the wrong way, and I imagined by the end of the night they'd wished they hadn't come.

"Speaking of the job, do you think we'll still get paid?"

"Honey, how tacky!" I wondered the same thing, but didn't say it out loud. She paid us an advance, but still owed several thousand dollars. That wouldn't be the first time, or the last, I'd associated "tacky" with Honey. She grew up in the mountains of North Georgia where country was cool. You can take the girl out of the country, but you can't take the country out of the girl. She lived in Vinings, not far from Mitch and me, and had worked as my right hand girl for years.

"Hey, I've never said I'm not tacky. Go on, tell the truth, aren't you worried?"

Honey married into money, but her social skills had never caught up. When I started my business, wanting to make a go of it on my own, I could only pay minimum wage. Honey volunteered to help. She didn't need the money, but her second husband had just died and she wanted something to keep her busy. I considered her a big asset, even if she exhibited a few rough edges. With Honey at my side, my business took off and not only prospered, but now I paid her a decent wage.

"I am concerned, but it's still not appropriate for us to worry about ourselves considering the circumstances. Hey, I need to finish getting ready, how about meeting for lunch at the OK Café?" This well-known eatery stood at the corner of West Paces Ferry Road and Northside Parkway. Barring heavy traffic it'd take us less than twenty minutes to get there.

The parking lot packed, I fought for a space, barely beating a little Mini Cooper. I guess I should've felt bad, but they say all's fair in love and parking lots.

I spotted Honey right away. Obviously, she'd shopped in the junior department again. She'd donned a sky blue dress that barely reached her knees. She paired the outfit with chocolate high-heeled boots. Being petite, she half-way pulled it off. Was I jealous? Just a little, but I remembered I wasn't a teenager anymore and didn't need to dress like one. My own outfit of brown pants and a beige blouse worn with ankle boots were more my style.

"Honey!" Headed in the same direction, I raised my hand and vigorously waved. She did the same and we arrived at the entrance simultaneously.

A myriad of delectable aromas greeted me as I entered. The OK Café was the place to go if you wanted down home, slap-yo-mama cooking, as Honey would say. Black and white fifties décor took me back to my childhood. The walls were covered in old 45 records and posters of singers from a time when a simple way of living still existed.

After a short time, a waitress wearing a white dress and a black and white checkered hat seated us in a booth with room enough to accommodate a family. We'd have plenty of elbow space. "May I help you ladies?"

"Skye, you order first, I want to study the menu." She put on her reading glasses and raised the menu.

I smiled at the waitress, Dorothy, according to her nametag. She returned my smile, but it didn't reach her eyes. I imagined her feet hurt from standing on them all day. "I'll take a vegetable plate with black-eyed peas, turnip greens, macaroni and cheese, and squash casserole," I watched her scribble on her notepad, "oh, and don't forget a piece of your cornbread." The cornbread at the café was to die for. She took Honey's order as well, stuck the pencil behind her ear, and retreated to place our order.

"What else did you hear about Sylvia?" I leaned in so others nearby wouldn't hear our conversation. The gesture flew right over Honey's head. When she spoke in her usual voice a gym teacher would covet, all eyes shifted in our direction.

"Well, I heard that her house was broken into. The police found the side door busted open. You know, John Abbot, the city councilman who lives next door to Sylvia?" I nodded and she continued, "He was the one who found her."

I sat back and shook my head. "How in the world did you find that out?"

"I've got my ways." She grinned like a Cheshire cat.

The waitress brought our food, and the conversation abated while we sated our appetite. Halfway through our meal, Honey looked over my shoulder and waved. "Over here, Amber!" I twisted and saw Amber Styles, our competitor in the decorating business. She'd decorated Sylvia's house several years ago, and she resented we'd redone her work.

"Honey! Don't ask her…"

Too late. Amber marched toward us like a scorned woman on a mission.

"Hi Amber." Honey was unaffected by Amber's stone-cold stare.

She fixed her stare on me. "Fancy meeting you here."

I didn't want a confrontation so I greeted her with aplomb. "Uh, hi Amber."

Before she had a chance to answer, Honey blurted, "Hey, did you hear about Sylvia?"

"Yes, I did. And after the way she acted last night I'm not surprised someone clocked the old biddy. Thought she had to cut everyone down to make herself look bigger. Except for y'all. Makes me wonder what you did to wrap her around your finger."

She looked me up and down. "Love your outfit. You'll have to let me know where you bought it." I didn't think she intended to buy one just like it. She directed her attention back to Honey. "And Honey, that was some story you spun about Blackbeard's writing table."

A most handsome specimen of the human race came and stood beside Amber. Her demeanor instantly changed, and she shot him a hundred watt smile. The smile disappeared when she addressed us. "Well, I've got to go." She offered a princess wave as she walked off with his arm around her waist.

"Wow, how did she snag him?" Honey shook her head. "I heard she's going to AA meetings. Maybe she met him there."

I leaned forward again, "AA? To meet men?" I mentally slapped myself on the wrist.

"That's not what I meant, but I wouldn't put it past her!"

I'm no goodie-two-shoes, but I tried to do what's right. More often than not, I missed the mark. Being around Honey made it hard at times. She was a walking gossip mill, which made it easy to blame her for being a bad influence, but I knew better. But knowing better, didn't keep me from struggling every day to keep on the straight and narrow.

"Never mind. Speaking of Blackbeard's desk, why did you spin that tale last night?" It was late when we'd left for home last night. We hadn't had a chance to unpack everything that had happened at the party.

"Well, you said rumors claimed Blackbeard owned it at one time. I just wanted to liven up the intrigue a little, and the distraction worked. Sylvia got way out of hand dissing everyone." Honey looked in her hand-held mirror and applied her Romance Red lipstick she wore year round. She smacked her lips together and blotted them on a Kleenex. I think Honey's the only person left on the planet that blots her lips.

I changed the subject back to our business at hand, more worried than I wanted to admit. "Listen, I've got to get that desk back to Mitch's warehouse."

"Why?" Honey asked. "He's got plenty of other pieces he can sell."

"I kind of borrowed it from the shop before asking his permission and now he has a buyer for it. I didn't think he'd miss it. I use artifacts from there all the time and tell him later, but he said a client called about that particular piece. He thought he'd stored it in the warehouse and he planned to look when he returned from his trip. I'm afraid if I don't get it back Mitch isn't going to let me use anymore of his pieces. And I rely on his expertise. Anyway, Sylvia said she didn't like it and wanted me to take it back."

"How are we going to do that? The police probably won't let us in." She nodded to the waitress acknowledging we were ready for our checks.

"Probably not, but I still have the key." I held it up to show Honey.

She shot me a grin. "I've got an idea."

"Oh, nooo." Honey with an idea was as dangerous as a stirred-up hornets nest. "What do you have in mind?" I waggled a brow, signaling for Honey to wait until the waitress refilled our tea glasses. I didn't know what she planned on saying, but the waitress didn't need to hear. We already planned to break and enter a crime scene.

Before Honey could speak, my phone played "Redeemed" by Big Daddy Weave. I rummaged in my pocketbook, pulled out the phone, and read the name. Mitch. "Hello, sweetheart. How are you?"

"I'm doing fine, but I've got some bad news. My plans have changed and I arrive home tomorrow morning." I could hear his disappointment. My husband loved to travel, but when he finished his business he wanted to come home to our condo on Peachtree Street.

"I'm sorry, hon." And I meant it. But my mind spun like a whirlwind of fall leaves. We'd take the opportunity to return the culprit desk back to the shop tonight. I cut the call short so I could tell Honey the news.

"Mitch has to stay another night and won't return home until tomorrow," I said.

"Stuck in airline traveler's vortex?" Honey shook her head.

"His misfortune is our opportunity. It gives us time to get that piece back and return it to the warehouse."

Honey's face lit up and I could almost see the light bulb over her head. "Let me tell you about my idea." She looked around. "Okay, it doesn't look like anybody's paying attention to us." She leaned in. "Remember those black tights we bought when we signed up for the gym?"

# CHAPTER TWO

I put my face in my hands. "Ohhh, please don't remind me." Although neither one of us were considered overweight, we'd decided the flab on our arms needed toning. That lasted all of six months. Honey got too busy, after she volunteered to help a friend taking cancer treatments, and I found it too hard to go alone. We started missing one day a week, two days, and before you knew it we'd stopped going.

"Well, I've got a good use for those tights." She squinted her eyes at me, "You did keep them didn't you?"

I nodded cautiously, suspicious of what she might suggest.

"We dress in black, sneak in after dark, and liberate the table. What happens at Sylvia's stays at Sylvia's. It won't be stealing, because you said she didn't want it and never paid for the desk." She sat back with a satisfied grin, like she'd just come up with a plan for world peace. I couldn't have imagined a proposal more bizarre.

"Are you out of your mind? How are we going to pull that off?"

"Have you got any better ideas?"

I had to admit I didn't. By the time we'd finished eating, we'd made plans to meet at Sylvia's after dark. I'll never know how I let her talk me into this. I spent the rest of the day worrying everyone I encountered could read my mind. Maybe Honey came from shifty ancestors, but I certainly didn't, and as a rule-keeper, I'd passed my comfort zone. But Mitch would have the last word if I didn't get that desk back!

That night, I tried on the tights combined with a long black sweater and a black toboggan cap belonging to Mitch. I looked in the mirror, and the image reminded me of a cat burglar. If Mitch saw me he'd have a heart attack. I had to admit, since I'd met Honey, she'd talked me into several adventures that resulted in disaster and Mitch questioning our friendship. I hoped this one didn't. I needed to get that desk back before he came home tomorrow.

We'd agreed to meet at Sylvia's, halfway between my condo and Honey's small cottage. I shut off the headlights as I drove the van up the driveway and behind the house where we'd load the desk. I got out and slinked around looking for Honey. The dark prevented me from seeing her. I didn't want to turn on the flashlight yet. My heart pounded at every little sound.

"Hey!"

I jumped out of my skin – well not literally. "What are you doing? I almost had a heart attack." I held my hand over my heart to calm the palpitations.

"Calm down," she whispered. "You're going to give us away."

"Where did you park? I didn't see your car." An owl hooted overhead, restarting my frenzied heart.

"Down the road. Didn't want anybody to see us." She looked at the van and shook her head. "A moot point, wasn't it?"

"I parked here because we have to load the desk. I think we'd draw suspicion carrying an 18th century writing desk down the road." I grabbed her arm and pulled her toward the back door. "Come on, let's get this over with."

"Okay, let's go!" Honey pulled on a pair of black lace gloves. She looked up at me, wiggling the fingers so the sequined trim twinkled in the moonlight. "What?" She looked at me incredulously. "I don't want to leave my fingerprints."

"Really? Our fingerprints are all over the house. We just finished decorating it."

"Oh, I knew that. I was just getting into character."

*Umhum, sure.* With shaking hands I fumbled the key into the lock. Until this moment I hadn't considered the possibility of an alarm. Honey stood so close, her hot breath tickled my neck. "Scoot back a little. I need some room."

The door squeaked open and I held my breath, but no horns honked, and no tell-tale beeping. We powered our flashlights and wound our way through the kitchen, the dining room, and into the living room. "There it is!" I stopped next to the small desk, sitting in the foyer, right where we'd arranged it.

"Wow, all the fuss over this old thing," Honey observed. "1800's?"

"No, at least mid-1700's. That's just it – it is exquisite and quite collectible. I don't know why Sylvia refused it. A lot of people would love to have it. Well, it's her loss." I spoke before I realized what I'd said. We were talking about a woman who'd lost her life. Possibly murdered. I wondered if the person who perpetrated the dastardly deed had hidden in the house. Just then, a floorboard squeaked overhead. Chills ran down my spine. Honey must have heard it, too, because she latched onto me with a vise-like grip. "Ouch!"

"Shhh, you're going to give us away. Let's get out of here."

I couldn't have agreed more. She clumsily held onto one end of the desk, her gloved fingers slipped several times. I had better luck on my end. We took a moment while she adjusted her grip, listening for more noises. Our plan proceeded without a hitch, until we came to the back door. Honey took the stairs down backwards and I followed. I started to remind her that last step was a doozy, when she lost her grip. The table jerked from my hands and toppled over the side. I heard a sickening crash.

"Oh, no!" I hurried down the steps and ran to the fallen desk.

"Well, you could ask if I'm all right."

"Oh, are you all right?" I flashed the light on her and found her with hands on hips. She looked fine to me. I wasn't so sure about the desk. The drawers had fallen out, and splintered pieces lay scattered.

"Hurry! Grab what you can and throw it in the van. We've got to get out of here before somebody calls the police." We bumped into each other, gathering as much as possible. I gave the area one last sweep with the flashlight, tugged the back door closed, and ran over to the van. I hopped in the driver's seat while Honey jumped in the passenger side.

We passed her car parked a couple of blocks down.

"Aren't you going to stop and let me get my car?"

"We'll come back for it after we patch up this desk, I need your help! Mitch is going to kill me."

# CHAPTER THREE

s I raced down West Paces Ferry Road, I thought my heart would pound right out of my chest. I didn't know why I'd let Honey talk me into this disaster.

"Slow down, Skye, you're going to get us killed or at least pulled over."

Good advice. I eased off the accelerator, slowing us down a little. "You're right. I need to gain control." I glanced in the rear-view mirror to see blue lights gaining on us. "Don't look now, but I think we're busted."

She turned around anyway. "Oh, no. I don't want to go to jail and have to wear those awful orange coveralls." Just as I pulled over, preparing my explanation for wearing all black and racing through the night with broken items stolen from a crime scene, the police car swerved around me and shot through the night. We both breathed a sigh of relief.

"Wow! That was a close one." I wiped sweat from my brow.

"Yeah, I thought they were after us for sure. Gets your blood pumping though!" She acted like getting chased by the cops was great fun.

"We're going to look suspicious carrying all these broken pieces into the condo. Why don't we take it to the store? That way we'll have the tools, and we can work on the broken bits." I slowed down now that we'd gained some distance from Sylvia's house.

"What are you going to tell Mitch?"

"I've decided to come clean and tell Mitch what happened. I feel guilty for being deceitful. You know what they say?"

In usual Honey style she asked, "What do they say?"

"You know, crime doesn't pay."

"Skye, it's not like we're real criminals. We just tried to get back something that belonged to you anyway." I had to admit putting it that way didn't sound so bad after all. A thought popped into my mind. *How easy it is to justify a wrong.* A twinge of guilt pulled at my conscience.

Silence bathed the rest of the ride as we contemplated our own thoughts. I opened the door of the van. When I saw the broken desk, my heart shattered into as many pieces. I didn't know if the desk was fixable, but it would never regain the same value as before the accident.

We carried in the poor thing and stood looking at the disaster in the harsh lighting of the workshop, located behind the store. Honey considered the glass half full. "It's not so bad." She picked up a drawer and the bottom fell off. A folded piece of yellowed paper fell out and drifted to the floor. "What's this, a treasure map?" She laughed at her own joke. As she unfolded the fragile paper, her eyes popped wide and her jaw dropped. "Skye, look! It *is* a treasure map!" She shoved it under my nose.

"I can't see it that close." I pushed her arm away so I could focus. Sure enough, it looked like some kind of map. "Spread it out over here, careful, it's so brittle." I laid it out on a table. A large X, just like you see in the movies, marked the center. The fragile document had the name Martinique inscribed in calligraphy across the bottom edge. The 'M' was all curlicued and embellished with colors.

Honey pointed towards the elaborate word. "Who's Martinique?"

"It's an island in the Caribbean." I placed my finger on the X. "See, this isn't far from the ocean. Here are some coordinates, too. Wonder what this means?" The map was so old the paper had torn along the creases.

"I told you Blackbeard owned the desk," Honey said.

"Well, I don't know about Blackbeard, but this certainly speaks of pirates. Or something nefarious." My nerves were taut like stretched out rubber bands. *Skye, what have you gotten yourself into?*

"What do you think we should do?"

"Let's show Mitch in the morning. Maybe he can determine if it's real." I couldn't wait for Mitch to get home, so I could show him the map. "Why don't you spend the night? You can support me when Mitch comes in."

"What do you want to do about the desk?"

"Good question. I guess I'll have to come clean and see if Mitch can repair it." Sweat trickled down my forehead and into my eyes.

"First, we need to get my car. Then stop by my house to pick up some clothes." Honey spun around showing off her cat burglar outfit. I agreed; we didn't need to upset Mitch any more than when he discovered our antics.

That night I tossed and turned dreaming I'd been arrested for breaking and entering. Mitch had texted me his arrival time, so I left for the airport before Honey woke up. I left instructions to make herself at home, even though she would've anyway.

I noticed him before he spotted me. Tall, dark, and handsome, even with graying temples, he walked among the other travelers seeking family and friends. A big grin spread across his face the minute he noticed me. We'd been married more years than I remembered, and I loved him more each day. Sure, we had our ups and downs as a couple, but we'd always made it through the rough spots.

"Hey, babe," Mitch greeted. The warmth from his hug traveled though my body. I reveled in the bliss.

"I'm so glad you're back." I grabbed his carry-on bag and rolled it while he carried his other luggage.

"Anything exciting happen while I was gone?"

Oh, boy, he did have to ask that question. "Uh, Sylvia Landmark died. Possibly murdered."

He slowed his stride. "What?" He shook his head in disbelief. "What happened? What about your job, were you finished? Had she signed off and paid you?"

I hesitated to tell him the part Honey and I played in our little escapade, but I wanted to do the right thing and come clean. I wanted his opinion of the map we found in the ruined desk, and he'd find out about our discovery sooner or later. He knew the legend of the pirate, but didn't really believe it. I wondered what he would say.

I fessed up about Honey and I retrieving the desk so he would have it for his customer. I thought I'd save the discovery of the map for when we arrived home. I wanted to watch his reaction when he saw it.

We were in the car now, and he'd taken the wheel. "What am I going to tell my client now that the desk is broken?" He looked over at me while we waited at a traffic light.

"Just blame it on me. Don't you have anything similar he can have?"

"That's just it. He specifically asked for *that* desk. Said he'd tracked it for some time and finally found out that I'd bought it at auction." He slammed on his brakes to keep from being hit by an SUV running a red light. Atlanta traffic, at its best, was hazardous to your health.

"What's his name?"

"Gill Brookhaven, he's a big land developer and collects antiques on the side. He was really interested in this particular desk. It's a great antique, but it surprised me he was so adamant about having it. I wish I'd kept the desk in the display store instead of putting it in the warehouse." He patted my leg. "I know how fond you are of picking out something for your clients and telling me later."

I breathed a sigh of relief. "You aren't mad at me?"

"Humph, I didn't say that." His twinkling eyes belied his sternness. "Nah, I'm not mad, but you've got to quit taking things and letting me know after the fact. Especially if you're going to smash them to smithereens before I can get them back."

That reminded me of the map, which might never have been found if we hadn't broken the desk. "I have something else exciting to tell you. I wanted to wait until we got home though. Honey spent the night with me last night and she's waiting on us to get back."

"I hoped we'd spend some time alone before I went back to work."

I waggled my eyebrows. "Alone time? I look forward to having plenty of alone time tonight."

"Tell me, what's so exciting."

"We're almost there. I want to show you because you'll never believe it unless you see for yourself."

We parked beside Honey's bright red Chrysler Crossfire, one of her late husband's toys. She ran out of the house wearing leggings paired with an extra-long shirt and ankle boots. She'd teased her blonde hair, and held it in place with a hefty dose of hairspray. She bragged she alone kept her hairspray company in business. I believed her. Yoo-hoo, girl, the eighties called and they want their hairstyle back!

I feared she'd spill the beans and tell Mitch about the map. I wanted to at least wait until he settled in. I shook my head hoping she'd get the idea. Her excitement wasn't about the map – the news was worse. "Guess what, Ginger's here! She's going to stay with me for a while." She shot Mitch a cursory look, "Hey, Mitch, welcome home." She turned her attention back to me, "Isn't that great? I'm going to help her find a new job. In the meantime maybe she can help us at the shop."

Ginger had followed Honey, her older cousin, to Atlanta, "to make her fame and fortune." She didn't have the opportunity to marry into money like Honey. As a matter of fact, she referred to herself as an exotic dancer.

# CHAPTER FOUR

Honey pulled me aside. "This is the perfect opportunity to do an intervention on Ginger. She's decided she wants to give up the nightlife but can't bust loose. How could I say no? I've prayed for this a long time."

Put that way, I admired Honey for wanting to help her cousin.

"I want to use this opportunity to help her find a new job."

Mitch accepted Honey's offer to help carry his luggage inside. "Remember, I want to spend some time with you," he said when she'd gone inside. He leaned over and planted a kiss on my lips. "I missed you."

I'd missed Mitch, too, but I wanted to show him the treasure map. When Honey and Ginger entered, dressed like the Bobbsey twins, I wondered if they were in a contest to see who dressed the most outlandish. Ginger wore a tight, short blue-jean skirt with a form-fitting top that didn't leave much to the imagination. Her heels were so high I'm surprised she didn't get a nose-bleed. I found myself being judgmental again, as I wondered how reformed Ginger really was.

I knew I'd need to work on this. Jesus surely didn't judge people on how they looked. I shouldn't either. I said a quick little prayer, *Father please help me to be less judgmental.*

"Hi, Ginger. I hear you're going to stay with Honey for a while." I wondered how long "a while" meant.

"Hi, Skye. It's sure good to see ya'. I just love your apartment."

"Thanks." I didn't correct her, maybe she didn't know the difference between an apartment and a condo. "This is my husband, Mitch."

He shook hands with her and left to unpack and shower.

"Isn't Honey a doll to let me crash at her place for a while?" Ginger's voice, deep and raspy, reminded me of someone who'd smoked for many years.

"Uh, yeah, Honey's a doll all right." The thought flashed in my mind that this might put a damper on our search for the origins of the treasure map.

"I've already told her about the map."

"Oh." *So much for keeping it a secret.*

"Didn't you already tell Mitch about it?" Honey bounced around like a kid waiting to divulge a big secret.

Mitch walked in wearing a fresh button down shirt and khakis. "Did she already tell me what?" He walked beside me and slipped his arm around my waist. "What's going on? Does this have something to do with the desk?"

"Sort of," I said.

First he eyed me, and then Honey. He knew us too well. "Okay, go ahead and tell me."

"It's a map, Mitch. We found an old map!" Honey sing-songed, "we think it's a pirate's treasure map."

He looked at me for confirmation. "She's right. It looks like an ancient treasure map. I'll get it."

As I walked out of the room I heard Ginger saying, "Can I help you find the treasure?"

I went upstairs to the master bedroom where Mitch's suitcase lay open on the king-sized bed. His jacket hung on the back of a chair. The familiar items evoked happiness. I grabbed the map and scooted back downstairs.

I shoved it toward Mitch, "See! It looks real. It says it's on the island of Martinique in the Caribbean. It even has an X that marks the spot." He reached out to take it. "Careful, the paper's already torn in spots."

"Oooh, look at that. I sure would've liked to have met some of those pirates. Maybe get my hands on some of their booty." I looked at Ginger with mouth agape. "You know, like Johnny Depp and all?" she added. "What?"

Mitch belly-laughed. I expected dealing with Honey and Ginger both, would take me on a wild ride. Mitch examined our discovery, gingerly positioning it one way and another. "Skye, I'm not an expert in cartography, but I don't think this is anything. Somebody probably put the drawing in the desk for a joke. I wouldn't take it seriously. Where's the desk? I'd like to take a look at it."

"We took it to the workshop to assess the damage," I said.

"I'll check it out when I get to work."

Mitch left me with Honey and Ginger while he escaped. Disappointment shrouded me when he didn't take more interest in the map. This could boost his business and mine.

"Shoot, Skye, I thought Mitch would jump with excitement." Honey took a sip of coffee she'd made while I went to the airport. I poured myself a cup.

"Yeah, me too." The strong coffee trigged a coughing fit. Honey and Ginger ignored me. They gulped the coffee like they were drinking Kool-Aid.

"Maybe the map's not real," Ginger said.

"Well, I think we should go to the police. It's real. I feel it in my gut." Honey scooted off the barstool and poured another cup of coffee. I'd have a hard time keeping up with her today.

"Great idea, Honey. Let's do it right now." I picked up the map and examined it again. "I think we should make a copy, just in case they want to keep the original."

"Let's go! Don't you just love a man in uniform?" The question was rhetorical, so I didn't answer Ginger.

"Yes, I do," Honey said. "Come on. Skye, we should go in your car since my Crossfire only has room for two." I wondered why anyone would want a car with only two seats. My Toyota Highlander wasn't sporty, but practicality outweighed stylish. Especially when hauling supplies and swatches for a decorating business.

*Lord give me patience and please hurry.* I knew I'd need it with these two in tow.

A middle-aged woman in uniform, sitting behind the counter, greeted us. "May I help you?" Her clipped speech matched the no-nonsense approach. Her short salt and pepper hair and stern expression exhibited an all business attitude.

"We'd like to see the detective on the Sylvia Landmark case." She looked at us like we were the suspects.

"Have a seat and I'll be right back." It took more than a few minutes.

"Okay, Detective Montaine will see you now. It's the second door on the left." Donna, according to her nametag, sat down as a dismissal of us mere minions.

I first noticed the beat-up, scarred desk. The well-worn piece of furniture looked out of place in the new office. The police station was part of a new city complex. I performed a double-take when I eyed the detective. He was the spitting image of Tom Selleck. Obviously, the resemblance had shocked Honey and Ginger as well. I'd rarely seen Honey speechless.

"Close your mouths ladies. I know what you're thinking. I've been told more than once I look like Magnum." He spoke with a South Georgia accent smooth as velvet. I saw the wheels turning in Honey's head. She'd look for a wedding ring first thing.

She turned to me and stage whispered. "He isn't wearing a ring."

The handsome detective cleared his throat. "How can I help you ladies?" He sat down in an office chair that squeaked under his weight. He leaned forward, placed his hands on his desk, and gave us his full attention.

We spoke at the same time. "Ladies! One at a time please."

I took the lead. "Okay, I'll play spokesperson. We were at Sylvia Landmark's house the night she died. We attended the party she gave to celebrate the remodeling of her house." I placed my hand on Honey's shoulder. "This is Honey Truelove, my friend and assistant at my decorating business Stylish Décor. I'm Skye Southerland."

"I know who you are. I plan on interviewing all of the attendees of the party in the next few days. Now why are you here?"

Ginger spoke up, "They found a treasure map."

Detective Montaine's dark chocolate eyes popped wide open. "Found a treasure map? Did you find it in the cereal box?" He guffawed at his own joke. His humor didn't amuse me. How were we ever going to get anyone to take us seriously?

I took the map out of my purse, laid it on his desk, and smoothed it out.

Ginger pushed me out of the way. "Oh, look at that. It has an X on it to show where the treasure is."

Well at least one person believed us. "The desk had resided in Sylvia's house for a while, but she wanted me to take it back. In the process of moving it we shifted the desk," I hedged the truth a bit, "breaking the drawer open, which exposed the map.

"Look ladies, I appreciate you coming in and bringing this and I'll sure keep it in mind. If I think it's relevant to the case I'll get back with you. I really don't see a connection." That's the best we were going to get from the good-looking detective.

# CHAPTER FIVE

**D**etective Montaine dismissed us by escorting us to his office door. We strode past Donna who gave us a cat that ate the bird grin. We traipsed out to my SUV where we contemplated our next move.

"Wow, what a hottie." I agreed with Ginger's observation, but I planned on keeping my thoughts to myself. Not so Honey.

"You've got that right! And it's just icing on the cake he's not married. Maybe we can find something else to tell him."

"Good grief, Honey, Sylvia's dead and that's all you can think about?"

Honey huffed and gave me the evil eye. "I'm foot-loose and fancy-free. Just because you're married to the love of your life doesn't mean I don't want somebody in my life that would love me the way Mitch loves you. And hopefully they wouldn't croak on me anytime soon."

"Yeah, what she said," Ginger agreed, nodding her head vigorously.

Honey often spoke her mind. This time I concurred with her. She'd married twice and both of her husbands had died. The outcome might have been different if she hadn't married men almost twice her age. She had a penchant for older men. I was glad to see her taking interest in a man closer to her age.

"I'm sorry, Honey. You're right; I'm blessed to have married the love of my life. We all agree the detective's a hunk, now can we get back to what we're going to do with the map?"

"I don't understand why nobody believes us. They won't even take a second look at the map." She shook her head.

My stomach growled like an angry bear. "Why don't we go to lunch and talk about it?"

"Yeah, I'm so hungry I could eat a possum," Ginger said. "Honey, remember the possum stew my Mama used to make? Ain't nothing better than a good bowl of possum stew."

"I remember, but I don't think that's what Skye had in mind."

My stomach roiled and all of a sudden my appetite took a nosedive. I had to redirect this conversation.

"Let's go to the Old Vinings Inn. That's a great little spot for lunch." I headed for Paces Mill Road and the quaint little restaurant located in a historic house.

"Ooh, that sounds like fun. I'd love to go to one of those fancy places Honey goes to." Ginger, riding shotgun, rummaged around in her purse and pulled out a mirror. She spiked her short hair and sprayed it, put on more blush, and applied lipstick. She now officially looked like an advertisement for make-up products. I believed every old barn needed a coat of paint now and then, but this barn received a double coat. I tried to ignore the pink streaks in her hair. I noticed how demure Honey appeared next to Ginger.

My stomach growled as we pulled into the parking lot of the Old Vinings Inn. Two young valets ran up and vied for the opportunity to park our car. I spotted a female valet – I gave her the keys.

I thought Ginger's eyes would pop when she saw the exquisite layout of the restaurant. In the main dining room bouquets of colorful spring flowers, in cut crystal vases, accented the round tables covered with white table clothes. The tables were set with fine china and cloth napkins. The waiters were dressed in black pants with white shirts and black bow-ties. Fine art paintings in ornate frames adorned the walls.

"Wow, what a snazzy place." Ginger rotated 360 degrees taking in the sight. "Honey, you sure live high on the hog." Like Honey, Ginger obviously didn't have a volume button. My face grew warm as her voice drew curiosity. I didn't like to draw attention to myself, even though I should have been used to it by now with Honey in tow most of the time. But I wasn't – now I had two attention getters to deal with.

Honey turned to Ginger, "It sure is snazzy. Just wait until you taste the food."

"Is it as good as Mama used to make?"

"Of course not, but it sure comes in a close second." When the maître d' asked us where we wanted to sit, I immediately suggested the deck. We enjoyed a beautiful spring day in May, the perfect time to sit outside – away from most of the diners. A stab of guilt pricked me. I needed to ask God to help me to accept the differences in each of his children.

My good intentions lasted all of five minutes when the waitress took our orders, and Ginger inquired if they had black-eyed peas and hog-jowls. Even Honey raised an eyebrow.

"Uh, Ginger, I don't think they serve those here. How 'bout aspara-gus with hollandaise sauce." I appreciated Honey attempting to rescue the situation, but she failed miserably.

"Asparagus, yuck! You know I don't like that green stuff." She made a face that would rival a kid asked to eat spinach. "How 'bout some good ole macaroni and cheese. You got any of that?"

Credit the young lady for keeping a straight face. I'm sure when she went back to the kitchen they had a good laugh. "Yes, ma'am, we do have macaroni and cheese with bacon in truffle sauce. It's one of our more popular dishes."

She screwed her mouth, and I braced myself, but nodded. "That's more like it. Bacon in macaroni and cheese. What's not to like? I want that."

After we finished ordering, I told the girls the history behind the building. The Old Vinings Inn dated back to the early 1800's making it one of the oldest historic structures around. Mitch and I loved coming to the Inn, and I thought of the many wonderful evenings we'd shared together.

"Dig out that treasure map and let's take another look at it." Honey pulled the lemon slice out of her water glass and plopped it onto the table. Ginger nodded, and I noted her napkin stuck in her collar.

*Way to go Honey, announce our secret to everyone within earshot. Honey and Ginger were going to be the death of me yet.*

"Shhh, people are listening." I pulled out the map and gingerly laid it on the table and smoothed it out. It looked like it might tear with the slightest tug. "Boy this is really fragile."

"I don't get why nobody believed it could be a real map. The detective didn't even want to keep it," Honey said.

We continued to discuss the validity of the map until the waitress served lunch. We talked in between bites and I'd relaxed, thinking we'd get through the rest of the meal without incidence. I should have known better.

# CHAPTER SIX

Eating outside had its drawbacks. The yellow jackets swarmed looking for a victim. Several of the pesky insects flew around while we ate. But what one of them did next led to a catastrophe I'd never forget.

One of them decided to fly down Ginger's top. She jumped up knocking the chair over backwards and macaroni and cheese went flying. "Oh, no! Oh, no! It's going to sting me!" Honey slapped at Ginger's top trying to rid her of the pest. I'm not sure what I would have done, but I don't think I would have chosen Ginger's technique.

"Oh, shoot! I'm not going to stand here and get stung." She yanked off her top before I could get up from my chair. I thought my heart would literally jump out of my throat. Thank goodness she had on a camisole.

Just when my heart slowed to a normal pace, in walked John and Stephanie Abbot. Ginger raised her hand and yelled across the deck. "Hi, John! How ya' doing?" I'd never seen anyone's face as crimson as John's. He gave a weak little wave and steered his wife away from us.

Ginger flapped her shirt to drive off the wasps, and finally put her top back on and sat down. I plopped into my chair. Honey sputtered, trying to say something intelligent. I found my voice first. "Where do you know John Abbot from?"

"Oh, John visits the club all the time," she said with a wink. "Don't you worry though. I'm no longer in the business. Honey showed me the error of my ways and she's going to help me stay on the straight and narrow. She's taught me about Jesus and how he wouldn't want me doing that anymore." She straightened one of her sleeves. "I have to admit it's not been easy to give up the good lifestyle, but with your and Honey's help I know I can do it."

*Did I just hear "you" and Honey?* When did I volunteer as a participant in this intervention? I didn't remember signing up for the job. Then it hit me, maybe I didn't sign up. Maybe someone with much more wisdom signed me up. Food for thought. That didn't keep me from embarrassment. I wouldn't see the inside of Old Vinings Inn for a long time.

We spent the rest of the afternoon at my shop working on our next job. Honey put Ginger to work, and I had to admit having an extra pair of hands around relieved some of my pressure. My back hurt from lifting the sample books all afternoon. I longed to go home and soak. A garden tub full of hot water and bubbles equaled a little bit of heaven on earth. I couldn't wait.

Honey left with Ginger in tow. I couldn't believe I'd lived through this disastrous day. I looked forward to Mitch waiting at home. I had the entire evening to spend with my sweetie.

I fixed a candlelit dinner for Mitch. We talked about the day's happenings and the enjoyment of spending the evening together. I took that bath I'd dreamed about and we turned in early.

We were asleep when Mitch's phone rang. I tried to make sense of the one-sided conversation. "Really? Yes. I'm on my way." He threw back the cover and swung his legs over the side of the bed.

"What's the matter?" I glanced at the digital clock on the bedside table. The numbers read 2:30 in the morning.

"That was the security company. The store's alarm went off and they've contacted the police. I've got to get there as soon as possible and assess the damage." He already had one leg through his jeans.

I headed to my closet. "I'm going, too."

"I don't think so. It's too dangerous."

"Mitch, I want to go. The police are there and I'm sure the perpetrators have left by now. Nobody would stay around with the alarm going off."

"Hurry," he said, grabbing his keys. I had enough time to throw on a pair of slacks and t-shirt while he backed the car out of the garage.

Police cars and a fire engine already surrounded the building by the time we arrived. It looked like a catastrophic event had taken place.

"My goodness, Guard My Property really does a good job. I think they've called everybody but the marines," I said.

Light from the surrounding buildings lit up the night. My heart skipped a beat when I noticed the shattered front window. The boldness of the perpetrator surprised me. Mitch's store held millions in inventory and I wondered what they'd stolen. He'd taken years to build his business and I knew what a robbery would do to him.

We identified ourselves while the officers checked the interior of the building. It took a while, but they finally asked Mitch to make an inventory of any stolen items. The next several hours we spent checking our list against anything missing.

When we were finished, he rubbed his chin and shook his head. "I don't get it. Nothing is missing but the desk. Who would steal a broken desk, better yet, why steal a broken desk? Who's going to believe this?" We headed for the officer who requested the inventory list.

"Hey, do you think this has anything to do with the treasure map?" Maybe this confirmed the map's validity. I itched to tell Honey.

Mitch shook his head. "I don't know, but I don't think so."

"Well, I'm going to call Honey. This might prove the map's real." I turned around to find a quiet corner to call Honey when I ran smack into a brick wall – named Detective Montaine. I sucked in my breath. Why did the officers call him in?

"Hello, Ms. Southerland." He removed his hat like a southern gentleman.

"Oh, Detective Montaine." I introduced him to Mitch. "I'm so glad you're here. Did you hear the only thing missing is the broken antique desk where we found the map? Doesn't that prove the map is real?"

"Whoa, there. I don't know if it proves anything. I do know, however, that since you were at the victim's house the night before her murder, I wonder if this break-in is connected." He placed his hat back on a head full of thick black Magnum P.I. hair. "I think it's time I interviewed you and your friend, Honey Truelove. Can you inform her I'd like to see both of you at my office later in the morning at eleven?"

"Uh, sure." Moisture bathed my hands and I labored to breathe. I didn't have anything to hide – well not counting sneaking into Sylvia's house and taking a piece of furniture from a crime scene.

"Okay. I need to speak with your husband now."

I pointed to where Mitch stood talking with one of the officers. I hurried and punched in Honey's number.

"I don't want any," Honey barked.

"Wait! Don't hang up!"

"Skye? Is that you?"

"Yes, I've got something important to tell you." Honey appreciated her sleep, but I also knew she'd want to know what had happened.

"It'd better be good." I heard a moan at the other end. "You've interrupted my beauty sleep."

"Listen. Someone broke into Antiques Emporium. The only thing missing is the desk. This has to mean the map is real."

A squeal pierced my ear. "I knew it! I knew it! Does Mitch agree now?"

"No, but it's only a matter of time. He'll come around. And Detective Montaine wants to see us at his office by 11:00 this morning to interview us about Sylvia's murder."

"Ooh, I can't wait to see him again. Ginger's going to be jealous. What should I wear?"

"Honey, it's an interview not a date. And I guess we need to come clean about taking the desk from Sylvia's, because if they investigate the desk's whereabouts it's bound to come out." I knew I needed to admit the truth, but I had a feeling his forgiveness wouldn't come as easy as Mitch's.

"You leave the detective to me. I'll turn on my womanly charms and have him wrapped around my finger in no time."

*Oh, Lord, save me from my friend's good intentions.*

"Ginger and I'll meet you there, or better yet let's meet for breakfast and go on over there." Honey rarely cooked. She usually ate out using the excuse cooking for one was too much trouble.

"Wait a minute, he didn't say anything about interviewing Ginger. Can't she stay at home?" My chest tightened, I didn't want a replay of yesterday's fiasco.

"No way, Skye. I promised I'd stick to her like glue. She's serious about giving up her profession and I'm committed to helping her." Well, I surely appreciated her wanting to help Ginger with this *problem* she had, but I didn't look forward to baby-sitting her for however long the reformation took.

"Okay, let's meet at the OK Café again. I'm starved! The police woke us up a little after two this morning." I looked down at my jeans and tee shirt and decided to stop by the condo first.

"I'll meet you there in forty-five minutes." I should've given myself more time. The drive took an hour by the time I pulled into the parking lot. I'd opted for a black pair of Ralph Lauren slacks and a white blouse.

Honey had on khaki capris and a silky red see-through top with a cami underneath. Her flip-flops sported a red flower on top. She'd applied her signature, Romance Red, lipstick as usual. Ginger wore jeans so tight I feared they would split when she sat down. Her choice of tops left little to the imagination. It was a toss-up who wore the most make-up. Oh-my-goodness. I looked around to see if I knew anyone.

"Hey there, Skye. Isn't it exciting about the break-in? I can't wait to see that hunky detective again." Ginger had the attention of the other patrons by now. She just smiled and waved. "Everyone sure is friendly around these parts."

The gum-smacking waitress showed us to our table and handed out the menus. She said she'd take our orders in a few minutes. Ginger, sitting next to the aisle, dropped her menu. She started to lean over and pick it up. I reached across the table and grabbed her arm. I feared *the girls* would pop right out of that top.

# CHAPTER SEVEN

"**L**et me get that for you, Ginger." I reached down and scooped up the menu.

"Why thank you, Skye."

The stress triggered a hot flash so I used my menu for a fan. Honey looked at me and smiled, "You having another power surge?" She slapped the table and laughed out loud. Her humor fell short with me.

After the waitress brought bacon, eggs, and toast, we talked about the map between bites. "Look," Honey said, "why don't we take it to someone who knows about maps. Maybe they can tell us if it's real or not."

"Hey, that's a great idea, Honey. Let's check for cartographers in Atlanta."

Honey's face scrunched up. "Cartographer?"

"Somebody who studies maps." I rummaged around in my purse and came up with my phone. "Let me see if I can find one." Sure enough, there were several listed. I picked the closest. "Here's a place near the condo. Let's check it out."

We finished our breakfast and left Honey's Crossfire in the parking lot and climbed into my Highlander. The Pawn Brokers inhabited a building on Peachtree located in a strip mall. A bell tinkled when I opened the door. Memorabilia covered the walls, every nook and cranny held objects from days gone by, and a glass-fronted counter boasted sparkling jewelry. I'd stepped into another century.

The man behind the counter looked like he'd stepped out of the Appalachians. I wouldn't want to meet this big burly man, with long brown hair and an even longer beard, in a dark alley.

"Howdy ladies, what can I do for you?" His gap-toothed smile belied his otherwise scary demeanor.

"I called and told you about the map we wanted you to look at." I hesitantly pulled out the document and handed it to him.

"Oh, yeah, I remember. Name's Samuel Baker." He reached over the counter and took the map from me.

"I'm Skye Southerland." I pointed to my two compadres, "These are my friends Honey and Ginger."

His eyes widened as he gave Honey and Ginger the once over. I shouldn't have been surprised when I caught Ginger giving him a little finger wave. I cleared my throat to get his attention back on the map.

"Uh, yes, the map. Can y'all give me about an hour? I need to study it before I give you an answer." He stroked his beard as he talked. I wondered what creepy-crawly things lived inside it.

Honey spoke up, "Sure. Why don't we go over to Lenox and shop for a while."

"Oooh, that sounds like fun," Ginger said. "Is there a Sears?"

I hesitated to leave it with him, but I didn't have much choice, and the sign in the window said he was bonded.

"How late do you stay open?"

"Six o'clock."

It was a quick drive to Lenox, but with heavy midday traffic we arrived twenty minutes later. I loved Atlanta, but hated the congestion that goes along with big city living.

Letting these two loose in the mall might prove more than my poor heart could handle, but I went along with the majority. I spent the next few hours trying to keep up with Honey and Ginger. I've never seen anybody who can spot a bargain from across the store like Honey. Even though she had plenty of money she rarely bought anything full price. Maybe this had to do with her upbringing. She mentioned several times how she didn't want to go back to a place she didn't know where her next meal was coming from. Once a month, she volunteered at the local soup kitchen to help others who had hit hard times.

As we walked down the hall, Honey stopped directly in front of me and I ran smack into her. Since I stood 4 inches taller and a good thirty pounds heavier, I almost knocked her down. "Sorry, Honey, but you stopped right in front of me."

"Look...Victoria's Secret. They're having a sale!"

That's not a place I usually shopped. I wore flannel pajamas most of the time. Honey grabbed my arm and pulled me in. Ginger followed, declaring Victoria's Secret as one of her favorite places. I had to admit, I found myself enjoying the heavenly scents displayed. I placed several different fragrances in my basket.

"Skye, come here." Honey yelled across the store. I hot-footed it over to where she stood so she wouldn't yell out my name again. "Look!" She held up a pink teddy. "Wouldn't Mitch just love this?"

"I know I would," Ginger said. I didn't doubt that for one minute. It hit me as ironic that we were shopping in Victoria's Secret while trying to perform an intervention on a woman that probably owned a chest-of-drawers full of lingerie.

Ginger grabbed the teddy from Honey and twirled around. "Isn't this just too cute," she said so loud her voice carried throughout the store. My ears warmed and my face probably turned a shade deeper than the teddy.

"Oh, come on, Skye. Lighten up. You need to put a little spice in your marriage. Look, I'll buy it for you as a gift. I promise it'll crank Mitch's tractor." I didn't know about Mitch's tractor, but if I didn't get these girls out of here I'd die of embarrassment. "I know a pretty gown always worked for Frank." Frank being Honey's late husband. At Frank's age I didn't know his tractor could still crank.

To speed up the painful process of getting them out of the store I acquiesced, "Okay, you can buy it for me."

"You mark my word, Skye, you'll thank me later." I pretended to admire a silk robe by the door while she made her purchases. With Honey and Ginger on my heels, I high-tailed it out of the store. They giggled as they planned a stop for pretzels and lemonade.

In reality, I wouldn't mind a little spice in our marriage. I just didn't want Honey and Ginger announcing it to the world. I'd been painfully shy growing up. The kids at school were well aware and took advantage of calling attention to me just to see me squirm. I'll never forget the time when Jimmy Edwards teased me for wearing two different shoes. I'll never understand how I left the house without Mother noticing, but I never let that happen again.

I'd grown more confident through the years, but occasionally an unpleasant event triggered the old feelings and they came rushing back. This was one of those times. I was glad the girls suggested we eat – I needed comfort food. We had a variety of places to choose from in the food court. Each one of us chose something different.

I finally distracted their minds by bringing up the mystery map. We excitedly chattered about going back to Samuel Baker's. When we left the mall and headed towards Pawn Broker's, it hit me that we'd forgotten to go by Detective Montaine's.

"Where ya' going Skye? This isn't the way back to the pawn shop," Honey noted when I turned left instead of right.

"I forgot the detective asked us to stop by. I hope he's not too mad at us for coming in late." I looked over my shoulder and scooted into the right lane.

The girls squealed. "Oh, I can't wait to see that hunk again," Ginger said and pulled out a pocket mirror and lipstick.

"Yeah, me too. Maybe if I hint around he'll ask me out." I admired Honey's ability to easily converse with someone she'd just met. Dialogue came natural for her, but I had to work to hold up my end of a conversation.

I moaned. "I don't think dating is his objective." We parked the Highlander and traipsed in the station again. Donna sat at the computer working hard. Her fingers tapped the keys like her life depended on documenting information in record time.

I cleared my throat and rang the bell. She looked up from her work and let out a big sigh. "May I help you? Again."

Honey spoke, "You sure can Sugar. We need to see Detective Montaine. Would you tell him we're here?" The authority in Honey's voice made her seem taller than her 5'2".

Donna changed her attitude right quick. "Sure. I'll let him know." We were waved back in just a minute.

Mr. Hunky sat at his work-worn desk, leaning back in his chair with hands locked behind his head. When we walked in, he jumped up and offered us a place to sit. "I see you ladies finally decided to come in."

"We got so excited about taking the map to a cartographer that we completely forgot the time," I said.

He sat on the corner of his desk and rubbed his hand through his thick black hair. I imagined Honey swooning and Ginger wiping drool from her mouth. "Oh?"

"Yeah," Honey said. "We're going to Mr. Samuel Baker's when we leave here to find out if it's authentic.

Detective Montaine stood. "Samuel Baker from Pawn Broker's?"

I scooted around in my seat trying to find a spot where a spring didn't poke me.

He gave a strange little grin and the hair on the back of my neck stood up as well. "Yes. Do you know him?"

# CHAPTER EIGHT

"**Y**ou could say that. Actually, most of the police department is familiar with Mr. Baker." Honey and I looked
at each other and I wondered if she, too, had concerns
about Samuel Baker's expertise now. Detective Montaine's booming
voice interrupted my thoughts.

"Okay, Ms. Southerland, I'll interview you first and you two ladies
can wait out in the lobby. I want to talk with you separately." I shot
Honey a desperate look. I needed her. She and Ginger were gone in the
blink of an eye, leaving me alone with the detective.

He dragged his rolling chair in front of me and pulled a small notepad from his pocket. "Go ahead and tell me about the party."

Once I started I let it roll. I listed everyone who attended and told
him Sylvia took a stab at everybody, metaphorically speaking of course.
I expounded about the pirate story Honey made up, and the possibility
we'd stumbled on a real map. He lifted his eyebrows at that remark and
wrote something down in his little pad. I didn't think he believed me. I
ached to prove him wrong.

Finally, he scooted even closer to me, placed his hands on his knees,
and looked me straight in the eyes. "Is there anything else you want to
tell me?"

I shook my head. "No."

"Let me help jar your memory. When you came in and told me about the map you found, did you fail to mention when you retrieved the desk from Sylvia Landmark's?"

I looked down at my feet. Caught! "I-I" gulping back a lump, I dug deep for the courage to admit our escapade. "You see, Sylvia never approved of the desk, and the piece was still in my husband's inventory…" I stumbled to explain myself. "I just took something that belonged to us." The last part ended on a higher note and I offered up a little smile to emphasize my innocence.

He didn't buy it. "Are you sure that's the only reason you went over there at night?"

I gulped. "Yes, absolutely, scout's honor. Are you going to arrest us?" I didn't possess the fashion savvy of Honey, but I knew the orange coveralls didn't come right off the runway.

"Not yet." He leaned back, arms crossed looking down at me.

I didn't know if he was kidding or serious. Either way, the butterflies in my stomach were doing somersaults.

"First, I'm going to interview all of the party attendees. Since the break-in at your husband's store, I'm wondering if there isn't some connection between Sylvia's murder and that desk. Just stay in town in case I need to talk with you again."

I had no plans to go anywhere. "Yes, sir."

"You can go now, and would you tell Ms. Truelove to come in?" A big grin spread across his face, and a twinkle shone in his eyes. I wondered if she'd placed some kind of spell on him.

Honey and Ginger were laughing as if they weren't sitting in a police station waiting for interrogation. "Okay, your turn now."

Honey fluffed her hair, "How do I look?" She placed a hand on her hip and struck a pose.

I smiled at her tenacity. "You look fine, Honey." She strutted down the hall to the detective's office. Ginger and I chatted the next few minutes. I learned more about her profession than I ever cared to. I jumped up when Honey walked down the hall with Detective Montaine following her.

"Okay, ladies, I'm through for now but don't leave the city. I may need to talk to you again. And don't compromise the crime scene again. Or I will have to arrest you." I hardly believed my eyes when I saw him wink at Honey. "I'll see you later."

When we settled back in the car I asked Honey, "What was all that about?"

"Well, he can't really ask me for a date while he's working on the case, but he did ask me to meet him for coffee in the morning. All business you know."

"Yeah, monkey business," I said.

"Skye, petty doesn't flatter you. You have your knight in shining armor. It's my turn." She reached in her pocket and pulled out her lipstick like she drew a gun from its holster. She pulled down the mirror on her side and painted her lips. Again.

I headed toward Peachtree and Pawn Broker's. I hoped we learned more about the map. What would it mean if the document proved real? Would it lead us to a pirate's treasure?

When we walked in, I hoped Samuel Baker's big smile meant good news. "Well, hello ladies."

"What's the verdict, Samuel?" Honey mirrored his smile. Samuel just stared at Honey, mesmerized.

I cleared my throat. "Mr. Baker!"

"Sorry, just enjoying the view. I know you're waiting to hear about the map, so I won't keep you waiting. I've got good news. From what I can tell, it's authentic. You have one valuable document on your hands."

Honey and Ginger squealed like teenaged girls at a rock concert. "I knew it! I knew it!" Honey grabbed Ginger and gave her a shake.

"A real pirate's map! Can we look for the treasure now?" Ginger literally hopped up and down.

Ginger posed an excellent question. Could the ancient document lead us to the treasure, now that we'd confirmed the authenticity of the map? I didn't feel comfortable talking about our plans in front of Samuel. I needed to get the girls out of there quick.

"Honey, don't you think we need to go? It's almost time for Mr. Baker to close up." Honey wasn't in any bigger hurry to leave than Samuel.

"Shoot, I don't mind staying open for you ladies." Even though he said ladies, he looked at Honey.

I grabbed her arm and pulled her toward the door. "We have to go. I need to stop at the shop before we go home."

"Okay, okay. You don't have to get your knickers twisted." Samuel guffawed.

"It wasn't that funny." I retrieved the map from Samuel, paid him a stipend, and headed to the car.

"Why were you in such a hurry back there?" Honey asked incredulously.

"Yeah, he seemed like a nice guy," Ginger chimed in.

"I didn't think it wise to talk about the map and where we found it in front of Samuel, especially if we're planning on trying to find the treasure." The fewer who knew of our plans, the better our chances to discover a connection between Sylvia's death and the map itself.

"You're probably right." Honey, riding shotgun, fidgeted in her seat. "Wow! Do you really think we can find the treasure and become famous?"

Ginger piped up from the back seat, "What about me? Can I go too?"

I really hadn't planned on her tagging along with Honey. Trouble times two. I tried to discourage her. "We don't even know where it leads to yet—"

"Why sure you can, Sugar," Honey interrupted, throwing me a look. "You know I'm not going to leave you alone while you're going through withdrawals. We don't want you back-sliding do we?" Honey crossed her arms. "Isn't that right, Skye?"

I nearly choked on my answer, "Yeah, I guess so, Honey." She'd made her decision clear. Ginger would shadow her for an undetermined time. I'd better get used to Ginger and her *unique* personality, I had agreed to help her out after all.

We had some catch-up work at Stylish Décor, so we swung by there after picking up Honey's car. I had a new customer who owned property on Lake Lanier. He'd seen Sylvia's home and called me. I was thrilled to have a new job to work on. I didn't like too much down time between customers.

I arranged to run out there tomorrow and check out the house. In the meantime, I wanted to straighten up and take inventory, I hadn't had a chance since Sylvia's big reveal party. We worked until around nine, and by that time the sun had set and left a world void of light. I shut off the lights and we stepped outside. The night had grown darker than a little black dress. Honey and Ginger were jabbering about going to a movie, but I longed for sleep. I reached inside my purse for my keys when something jabbed my side.

"Honey, quit poking me, I told you I'm too tired, I just want to go home." The voice that answered certainly didn't belong to Honey.

# CHAPTER NINE

"**S**top right there, I've got a gun on you." He proved it by sticking the barrel deeper into my side. "Turn around slowly, and don't make any fast moves." I complied and saw Honey and Ginger bathed in moonlight, with their mouths agape. "All right, you two, over here by your friend." He waved the gun for them to move closer to me. A ski cap pulled down over his mouth muffled his voice.

Honey spoke up. "What do you want? I have money. Just don't hurt us." She shoved her purse toward him. "Here."

"I don't want your money," he growled, "You know what I want."

I spoke with false bravado. "No, I don't know what you want. Why don't you just tell us?"

"Don't be a smart-aleck lady." He waved the gun around like his arm was connected to a ceiling fan. Something about him seemed familiar. "Hand over the map." My heart skipped a beat and Honey gasped.

"There goes my chance to find a pirate's treasure," Ginger said.

I tried to open my satchel to get the map, but my hands shook so bad it took me a minute. Suddenly, I remembered what else I had in my bag. I grabbed the rolled up plans instead and shoved them toward him. A loud bang rang out, and the perpetrator crumbled at my feet. The gun clattered to the pavement. Honey and Ginger screamed. I swayed and my vision blurred. A wave of nausea hit me. In a matter of seconds another man wielding his own gun stood over the lifeless figure of the first guy.

"Hand the map to me." He stood, feet apart and his gun rolled sideways. He'd done this before.

"Good grief, how many people know about this map?" Honey clung to Ginger.

"Shut up and hand it over." He spoke to them, but looked at me.

I didn't wait for him to tell me twice. With shaking hands I handed him the plans. "You'd better not move from this spot for at least ten minutes. I have my way of knowing, and if you move I'll return to finish the job." With that he fled into the inky night. I don't think any of us could have moved if we'd wanted to.

"Lord please help us." Honey squeaked and looked heavenward after his footsteps receded. "Did you give him the real map or the copy?"

"Neither one," I gulped, "I gave him a set of plans."

"At least this confirms the map's real, because who would stick us up for a fake?"

She had a point. "We've got to call 911." I reached into my purse and brought out my phone. I pushed the numbers with trembling fingers. The operator assured me they'd send somebody right away. I called Mitch next.

"Skye, get back in the store, lock the doors, and wait for the police to arrive. I'm on the way." I hoped he'd drive fast – I needed him. I wanted to feel the warmth of his arms around me. I needed to feel safe.

We went back inside, and flipped on all the lights. After a few minutes, a sedan drove up outside, and a man in slacks and a button down shirt stepped out. Honey used her reflection in the window to primp as soon as she spotted her target. I guess I shouldn't have been surprised Detective Montaine showed up. A patrol unit also arrived, and two uniformed officers jumped out, listened to the detective for a moment, and nodded. He headed for the door. "What are you doing here?" I said when he'd stepped inside.

His eyes opened wide. "I think the question is what are you doing here?" He removed his hat and ran his hand through his hair before replacing it. Must be a nervous habit. About that time, the door opened and Mitch walked in. I ran into my husband's arms.

"Oh, Mitch, it was awful, just awful. I thought he'd shoot us." I hugged him with all my strength.

"Yeah, I was sure we were goners," Ginger said. She gave a little wave to the detective then looked outside at the other officers. They stood next to the body of the first stick-up man. She waved through the window, "Oh, hi Charlie. Hi Doug." One of them waved back. *Did she know the whole police department?*

Detective Montaine asked if we were all right. After making sure we weren't hurt he went back outside to where the dead man lay in a crumpled heap. He shone his flashlight around the victim.

Even though Mitch had his arm around me I feared my wobbly legs wouldn't hold me up. I shivered even though the night air felt warm. Honey and Ginger were huddled so close you couldn't fit a toothpick between them.

We followed the detective outside. "Stay out of our way. I have more questions," Detective Montaine said. We followed at a distance, hanging near the steps into the parking lot, the lights strobing the walls around us.

Montaine bent down, removed one glove, and felt for a pulse. A siren blared from the street, and the uniformed cops waved an ambulance over. Several EMT's ran over and knelt beside Detective Montaine. He shook his head. "No need to hurry boys. He's already gone." He stood up and looked around. "Hey, Charlie, call the ME and tell him to get down here right away. And forensics."

Detective Montaine looked our way. "Ladies, come over here a minute." I hesitated but followed Honey and Ginger over to the lifeless body. "Do you recognize this man?"

"It's Samuel Baker!" I gasped. "We just spoke with him this afternoon. He must have overheard our conversation."

"He demanded the map," Honey said. She moved a little closer to the detective. "But Skye gave him a set of plans instead."

Ginger moved a little closer to Honey. "And I thought he was such a nice man."

I had to admit I never saw this coming. Certainly, the attempted robbery and murder confirmed the map held value.

"Ms. Southerland. May I call you Skye?"

I nodded my head. "Sure."

"Skye, can I use your shop to talk with y'all? I need to find out what I can about this other man."

"Of course you can, Detective Montaine." I led the way into the shop. The familiarity of my workspace comforted me. I held onto Mitch's hand like he was my lifeline.

The detective spent the next half hour going over what we recalled from the day and into the evening. I told him about substituting the plans for the map. I didn't want the map, so I gave it to Detective Montaine. I still had the copy.

The more the detective spoke, the more I believed he connected Sylvia's death with the map. Had the events of the evening convinced him to believe us? Someone was willing to kill, more than once, to get their hands on that map. I shook like a leaf in a fall wind.

"What's the matter, babe?" Mitch hadn't left my side since his arrival.

"I was just thinking that at least two people were after the map." I narrowed my eyes. "Now, do you believe there's something special about our discovery?"

"I'm sorry I didn't listen to you, but I really didn't believe the map was authentic. I should have checked it out. Forgive me?" Mitch gave me a quick kiss on the cheek. "I couldn't stand it if something happened to you."

"You're forgiven." I shot him a smile. I knew he'd never purposely put me in harm's way.

Eventually, the detective released us to go home, but wanted to talk to us again first thing Monday. I wondered if he and Honey would still meet for coffee in the morning.

"Hey Skye, is it all right if Ginger and I spend the night with y'all? I don't wanna' go home."

"Sure, y'all come on over." Honey and Ginger would have to share a room since we only had two bedrooms, but being cousins I was sure they'd approve the arrangement. "Do you mind sharing a bed?"

"Nah, that's not a problem."

We hadn't eaten since lunch and were starving, so we decided to stop at IHOP. We arrived a few minutes before midnight. Our waitress, Jenny, possessed a face covered in wrinkles. The order of cigarette smoke clung to her clothes. She looked tired and life-weary, but when she smiled her face lit up.

"Hi there, how can I help ya?" She placed two coffee carafes on the table. "This one's high test and the other is decaf." She poised her pad ready to take down our order.

We ordered breakfast. I thought the excitement had killed my appetite, but it had the opposite effect on me. I shoveled in several bites before I took a breather.

"Wow, you okay Skye? I've never seen you put it away like that," Honey said. I'd finished half my pancakes, while Mitch had barely started.

I looked across the table and discovered the girls staring at me. "What? Haven't you ever seen anyone enjoying their meal?"

Honey help up her hands palms out. "Don't get defensive. I think you just have a bad case of nerves. We all do. I've never been so afraid in all my life."

"Yeah, me too. I've been in some scary situations, but I've never had a gun pointed at me," Ginger said. "What about y'all?"

I involuntarily imaged Ginger in some precarious situations. "No, I've never been held at gunpoint before."

"Me neither," Honey said. "Since there's evidence the map's connected to Sylvia's murder, we're considered persons of interest. Everyone at the party is. It doesn't look good for us, Skye." Honey shook her fork at me. "I told you it probably wasn't a good idea to take the desk from a crime scene. Really puts a damper on my budding relationship with Robert."

 hat! You did not!" I couldn't believe she threw me under the bus, and with Mitch sitting right there.

"Skye?" Mitch held his coffee mug mid-sip. "Is that true?"

"Well, it was my idea to get it back, but Honey came up with the hair-brained scheme to dress like cat burglars and sneak in at night." I knew the excuse fell flat. "You said you needed it for a client, and I didn't think it would do any harm to get it back since she didn't want it."

He shook his head and tossed his napkin on the Formica. "Ladies, it's late and everyone's last nerve has been stepped on. How about we go home and get a good night's sleep and we can discuss this again tomorrow." He directed the last comment to me.

We rode home in heavy silence. I dozed off and jerked awake when Mitch stopped the car. He gently placed his hand on my shoulder. "Skye, it's time to go in." He came around the car and opened the door for me. Home looked mighty good.

Once inside, Honey sidled up to me and whispered, "I guess this isn't a good night to try out your new teddy?" A grin spread across her face. Instead of giving her a piece of my mind, I wanted to throw the shopping bag at her. But she redeemed herself just in time.

"Just kidding!" She laughed like she'd just told the funniest joke ever. "Come on Ginger, we'd better go before Skye kills me."

I don't think she saw me roll my eyes, but what a bad choice of words. I slept fitfully. Dreams plagued my sleep. Men in ski masks surrounded me and demanded I hand them the Victoria's Secret bag. I kept pulling out pancakes and carpet samples and they yelled as if they were going to kill me like they did Sylvia. I sat straight up in bed.

"Skye, are you all right? You yelled out in your sleep." Mitch reached over and pulled me into his arms. Tears slid down my face as I basked in his warmth. I told him what I'd dreamed and we laughed about it. I apologized again for my slip up taking the desk from the house, and hoped the detective would forgive me as quickly as my husband. I slept the rest of the night snuggled against Mitch.

We slept in a bit, and over a light breakfast we decided to go to church. Ginger hesitated, but Honey convinced her to attend. We arrived as services at the Holy Ground Community Church were just beginning. People looked at us as we followed the usher down front to the only empty seats left.

After the sermon, several parishioners surrounded us on the front lawn. The holdup and shooting were front page news in the local paper. Someone showed me a very unflattering picture of myself lit up like a ghost in the harsh forensics work light. Nearby, Ginger and Honey chatted with some other folks I knew from our Sunday school class. Ginger, in her mini-skirt, high-heeled boots, and pink hair, attracted attention, but most welcomed her with opened arms and asked her to come back. She smiled and held her head a little higher.

Back in the Highlander, she observed, "The service wasn't so bad. I might even go back with you, Honey."

The rest of the day passed without incident. Honey and Ginger decided to go back to their house for the night. I endured another sleepless night wondering what Detective Montaine had planned for our meeting, since he considered us suspects. We planned to meet at the station at ten in the morning.

I awoke with flickers of light dancing through my window. The warmth of the rays filled me with a burst of energy. I scrambled from the bed, threw a robe on over my new nightie, and stuffed my feet in fluffy slippers. The smell of bacon, wafting through the air, along with the aroma of coffee drew me downstairs. Mitch had cooked breakfast.

"Hi, sweetie." He planted a kiss on my lips.

"Wow, the food smells wonderful. You cooked this for me?" I grabbed a piece of crunchy bacon and munched on it while I poured us coffee.

"You've been through a lot." He winked at me. "Let me spoil you a little."

We sat at the kitchen table of mosaic marble. A great example of how I felt. A kaleidoscope of colors. Still shaken from Saturday night, I had more questions than answers. How were the map and Sylvia connected? Did someone find out the desk had been in her house for a period of time?

"Hon!" Mitch's voice brought me back to earth. "Where did you go?"

"I was just thinking about Sylvia's murder. Did she really lose her life over the map, or was there something else going on in her life?" I shuddered at the implication for me and Honey. The person who stole the map last night must have been Sylvia's murderer. Would he come back for us? Especially if he figured out we had a copy?

"Why don't you come to work with me?"

"We're supposed to see Detective Montaine this morning. Anyway, I don't think they'll return." I displayed false confidence, but I didn't want Mitch to worry.

My phone rang and I scooted the chair back to answer it. "Good morning, Honey," I said.

"Hi, Skye. How ya' doing this morning?"

"Still a little shaky. How about you?"

"I feel better than I did yesterday. I'm just glad it's morning. Everything looks better in the daylight. You about ready for our interview with Robert?"

*Robert?* "Since when did you start calling him Robert?" I couldn't help but tease her a little about it. "Well, it's about time to leave if we're going to make it by ten. I'll see you there?"

"With bells on. I'll bring Ginger, too. It looks like she's mixed up in this right along with us. I'm sure sorry I got her involved. I was trying to keep her away from the police, not throw her to the wolves."

I believed Ginger could take care of herself when it came to the police. "Okay, I'll see you there." I threw on a teal blue skirt with a white tee and topped it off with a wide yellow belt. The outfit shone bright, but I needed cheering up.

I pulled in the parking lot right behind Honey. She stepped out of her little red car wearing orange capris with an orange and yellow pull-over blouse. Her orange clutch and orange Yellow Box flip-flops matched her outfit. She'd pulled her blonde hair into a ponytail and a pair of white sunglasses with black polka-dots sat atop her head. She looked as sporty as her Crossfire.

Not so, Ginger. Her lavender knit mini-dress fit so well, it left nothing to the imagination. If Ginger was attempting to start a new way of life, she would need to dress a little less like a call girl. I'd talk to Honey about it later.

We entered the police department as a couple of officers came out. They gave Ginger the once-over. Yep, I knew we'd have to do something about those clothes, or rather the lack of.

Donna sat behind the counter as usual. "I'll inform Detective Montaine you're here." She didn't scowl at us. Maybe she'd heard about our harrowing experience and cut us a break. Whatever the reason her new attitude became her.

We waited a few minutes while the detective finished a phone call. "Ms. Southerland come on back." I obediently followed him down the hall. He leaned forward, elbows propped on his scarred desk. "I'm sorry you went through that terrible experience and I didn't listen to y'all earlier when you brought the map in."

"No worries, all is forgiven." I hoped he'd remember my gracious reaction later when the desk-napping incident came up again.

"Under the circumstances, we'll consider the map authentic and that it was connected to Sylvia Landmark's murder." He asked me several more questions and confirmed what I'd dreaded. "I'm going to interview everyone who attended the party the night of Sylvia's murder. Since you have a connection to the map and you took the desk from a crime scene I have to consider you and Honey prime suspects."

He showed no pleasure in telling us. I had a feeling he'd fallen for Honey, putting him between a cactus and a porcupine. I knew our questioning was inevitable, but never expected we'd earn the title of main suspects. *Dear Lord, please help me out of this mess.*

Next, he talked to Ginger, and then asked Honey back to his office. He kept her twice as long as he did us. I heard Honey giggling like a lovesick teenager as they came down the hall. Whatever *Robert* said must have been very funny.

"All right ladies, I'm through with you, but don't plan on traveling for a while."

"Don't worry, I'm not going anywhere," Honey said. I think she meant that in more ways than one.

"How about we get something for lunch?"

"Why don't we go back to the condo and make some sandwiches?" As much as I loved going out to eat I didn't feel like being around a crowd of people.

"Oooh, that sounds like a great idea," Ginger said.

"I'll meet y'all there." Traffic flowed, so I made it in good time. I had the ham and bread out by the time the girls arrived. I made sandwiches and served potato-salad and baked beans. I called Mitch to see if he wanted to eat with us, but he said he needed to do some work at the shop.

Ginger talked between bites. "What a bummer about y'all being suspects and all. Too bad we don't have the map anymore."

"Well, that's not exactly true," I said. "Honey, remember when I made a copy of the map before we took it to Detective Montaine?"

"Of course!" Honey grabbed another sandwich from the platter. That girl ate just about anything and didn't gain a pound. "What should we do with it? Could we really use it to find a treasure?"

"I'd love to try, but maybe we need to wait a while and see what happens. We probably need to figure out what we're going to do about being suspects."

"Hey, I've got an idea," Honey said.

# CHAPTER ELEVEN

**O**h no, not another one of Honey's hair-brained ideas. "Honey, you remember what happened last time you had an idea. We almost got arrested for breaking and entering."

"No breaking and entering this time, I promise." I pointed to her chin and she wiped off a speck of mayonnaise. "I think the killer's someone who attended the party. Let's make a list of all the people who were there and do our own detecting." She laid down her cloth napkin and grinned like she'd just solved the world's problems.

"Let's go for it. I know a little about police work," Ginger said.

I wasn't surprised. "Come on, Honey. Do you really think it's a good idea to poke our noses into other people's business?"

"We've got to do something and who better than us since we were there. We need to save our own skins! I can't stand by while we're accused of a murder we didn't commit."

"We probably need an attorney." I retained one who helped me with my business incorporation, but doubted she practiced criminal law.

"A lawyer's going to ask all the same information, so we might as well get started."

"Okay, I'll get some paper and we can make a list of the party-goers," I said.

I went into Mitch's office and found paper and a pen while the girls cleared the table to make room.

"Honey, how about you write down the names." She grabbed the pen, ready to write. We shouted out the names we remembered.

1. *Amber Styles – Sylvia's previous interior decorator*
2. *Bernadette Jackson – Sylvia's housekeeper and assistant*
3. *Abigail Smith – Sylvia's cook*
4. *Raymond Smith – Abigail's husband and Sylvia's driver*
5. *Joan Landmark-Newton – Sylvia's daughter*
6. *Will Newton – Sylvia's son-in-law*
7. *Raphael Hadley – Sylvia's hairdresser*
8. *John Abbot – Sylvia's next door neighbor and city councilman*
9. *Stephanie Abbot – John's wife*
10. *Madeline Palmer – Sylvia's bridge partner*
11. *Elizabeth Herring – Sylvia's bridge partner*
12. *Gloria Habersham – Sylvia's bridge partner*

"Wow. That's a long list. We'll need to determine if any of them had a motive to kill Sylvia. Where they after the map or did they have another motive for killing her?" I made eye contact with Honey. "If we're going to get these people to talk to us we need a reason to give them."

"Why not just tell the truth," Ginger offered. "You can tell them you're the prime suspects for the murder and you're doing your own investigatin.'"

"I guess that's a possibility. What do you think Honey? Good idea?"

"Sure, we can give it a try. While we're here, let's take a look at the copy? Maybe it'll give us some clues."

I went back upstairs and discovered the map undisturbed. I breathed a sigh of relief, thankful I'd made a copy. I never dreamed a gunman would hold us up. *Now who did Mitch say asked about the desk before I took it to Sylvia's?* Maybe he had something to do with the hold-up.

"Here you go girls." I put the map on the table and we bumped heads getting a look.

"Okay, we know the treasure's located on Martinique. Here's a cliff marked on the north side of the island." Honey pointed to the cliff.

"Look here, there's something on the side of the cliff. Let me get the magnifying glass." I grabbed the magnifier from Mitch's office and hurried back to the kitchen. I leaned over and tried to decipher the design. "Woo hoo! It looks like a skull. Look." I handed the glass to Honey.

"Well I'll be hog-tied. It sure does."

Ginger grabbed it next and gave it a good look. "I see it, too." She pointed to the skull. "Look, here's something on top." She looked closer and declared, "It's a rock formation and it looks just like a …"

"Don't say it Ginger!" I blurted it out.

"What? I was going to say nose. Nose!" Ginger looked incredulous.

"Oh, sorry. Give me the magnifying glass." I grabbed the glass and took a gander. Sure enough it looked like a giant nose.

"This is great! Why can't we go and try to find the treasure?" Honey took another long look herself, combing over the entire piece of paper.

"Can't until we clear our names. Detective Montaine told us not to leave the area."

"And, we have to hurry up so I can go out with Robert." Honey's eyes had a far-away look to them. I understood why she fell for the Tom Selleck look-alike. But I wondered if he was friend or foe.

Ginger's eyes had the same dreamy look, "Yes, isn't he a hunk?"

"Earth to Honey! Earth to Ginger! You two need to get your mind back on saving our hides." They watched me pull out my cell. "I'm going to call Mitch and find out the man's name who wanted that desk. I wonder if he's involved. Oh good heavens, look at the time. We have to get out to Lake Lanier and talk to our new customer."

Honey's eyes lit up like the sun coming out after a summer rain. "Great, why don't we have some fun while we're there? We need a little R&R. Ginger can see if she's interested in a job on the island. We need to scout out some of the tourist's sites around Atlanta for employment opportunities. And have fun while we're looking – a win-win situation."

"Yeah, I'd love to have some fun. I love excitement, but not the kind we've had lately." Ginger laughed a deep throaty, smoker's laugh.

"Come on, girls. I'll call Mitch on the way to Lake Lanier." After I tucked the map away in a safe spot, we grabbed our pocketbooks and headed out the door. I'd locked up when the landline rang. I ran back inside and snatched the receiver. "Hello?"

"Hi, babe." Mitch! I told him to hold on and gave the girls a heads-up.

"I just called to say I love you." I knew Mitch really called to check on me.

"Love you back. And don't worry, I'm doing fine. We're fixing to drive out and meet my new client." I jiggled my keys and stopped when I remembered something. "Hey, could you remind me of the man's name who wanted to buy the desk?"

"It's Gill Brookhaven. Why? You and Honey aren't cooking something up are you? Detective Montaine has this under control and I'm sure he doesn't want you butting into his investigation."

"Mitch, he said we were the prime suspects because we took the desk. I can't sit by and let the real killers get away with murder."

"What do you have planned?"

The horn tooted, and it gave me the excuse I needed. "I'm sorry. Gotta' go. The girls are waiting for me. Love you. Bye." I felt a twinge of guilt for cutting him off, but I didn't want to tell him our plan. He'd just worry.

I locked up and hopped into the driver's seat. "Here we go." Honey rode shotgun. "His name is Gill Brookhaven."

"Who's Gill Brookhaven?" She pulled down the mirror and applied her, Romance Red, lipstick with an exaggerated swoop.

"The man who wanted to buy the desk. Remember, he came by the store and asked for that particular piece. He knew Mitch had bought it at auction."

"Maybe he'd heard about the hidden map," Ginger piped up from the back seat.

"Yeah, that's probably right." We accessed I-85 going north, and headed to State Road 985 that would take us right to Lake Lanier. The drive is about forty-five minutes, barring a traffic jam. This had always been a favorite get-away of mine and Mitch's. Sometimes we'd take a weekend off with no phones. Just spend time alone with each other. The respite rejuvenated our marriage.

The traffic moved smoothly. When we arrived, I checked the time and noticed my mistake. We still had a couple of hours to kill. There were a lot of things to do on the island for entertainment. "What do y'all want to do? We can ride horses, play miniature golf, go to the spa, or hike on the trails."

Ginger piped up from the back, "Let's ride horses. I've never done that before."

"That sounds like fun," Honey said. Honey had never ridden either.

Why did I suggest riding with two greenhorns? "Uh, you sure you want to ride? How about miniature golf?" A massage sounded wonderful. "I vote for the spa."

"Sorry, Skye, two against one, we win this round." Honey's laughter filled the air. "Won't I look cute on a horse? I wish Robert could see me."

Oh-my-goodness she had it bad. Fortunately, I had an extra pair of Lee jeans, in the car, I could change into. We pulled up to the parking area near the barn and the girls jumped out before I stopped the car.

# CHAPTER TWELVE

"Hey, wait on me!" They were halfway to the barn before I opened door. When I walked closer, I heard Ginger squeal as she ran to a stall. We checked in and learned we had a few minutes before the next group would leave for a ride on the beach. The tours left on the hour – I had plenty of time to change.

While I changed, Honey and Ginger received a quick riding lesson. Honey drew a pretty little Buckskin named Chief and Ginger an Appaloosa named Lightning. I hoped Ginger's horse didn't live up to his name. I wound up on a Bay, with a jet black mane, named Apache.

When the wrangler helped Honey she flew right up and into the saddle. Her feet barely reached the stirrups. Ginger didn't fare so well. It took three tries before she heaved herself astride. I don't think I'd ever seen a bigger smile.

Before we left, we listened to safety instructions. Our guide asked first time riders to practice in an enclosure for a few minutes. Ginger's horse didn't neck rein very well, so she had to pull in the direction she wanted Lightning to go. I looked over to see her going around in circles. "Try the other way Ginger, before you get dizzy," I hollered.

She pulled the other rein and wound up going in circles in the other direction. I imagined a *fun* ride. I reined my horse close to Ginger and tried to explain how to direct the horse. Finally she had him going straight.

"Aw this ain't so bad," Ginger said. Famous last words. When we were a little way from the barn, her horse ignored the reins and galloped back to his stall.

Dale, one of the leaders, rode up beside Ginger and grabbed Lightning's bridle. "Sorry ma'am, but this guy's a little barn sour. Don't let the name scare you, he won't run away with you. He's named for how fast he eats. By the time the barn's out of sight, he won't give you any trouble." Dale kept his horse right by Ginger's side.

Honey fared a little better with Chief. Her only problem was bouncing up and down when Chief trotted down a slope. Soreness would haunt us tomorrow. I knew what I was in for, but the girls didn't. I felt for them. Finally, we made it to the beach. I experienced God's beauty and peace, riding in the sand, watching the water lap toward the shore. Even though I had misgivings, the ride was just what I needed.

Honey and Ginger walked a lot slower back to the car. "Well girls, are you glad you rode?" I laughed as they whined about being sore.

"Yes, even if I can't walk tomorrow, the ride was worth it," Honey said.

"Yeah, the ride was fun, but meeting Dale was even better. He asked for my phone number. I told him I was taking a break from dating, so he gave me his number and told me to call him when I'm ready."

I wondered how long Honey planned on being Ginger's babysitter, but didn't say so. "Let's get something to drink and head over to Randall's house." We found a little place inside the Lodge called the Butler's Pantry. We treated ourselves to a cherry pastry and a Coke.

"There it is!" We found Lakeview Drive and spotted Randall's house, a beautiful cottage on the shore with a spectacular view of the lake. I couldn't wait to get my hands on this little beauty. I pulled into the driveway behind a sea green Volvo.

"Wow, look at this place. What I'd give to have a house like this," Ginger sighed.

"It is cute. Mitch and I talked about buying a home on the lake. We love to come here for a weekend get-away."

"Oh, and Honey and I can come visit. We'll have great fun." Ginger had quickly warmed her way into my life. I liked having her around, quirks and all.

Honey just laughed. "That's right. We could come and spend the weekend with you and even go horseback riding again." She grinned a Cheshire cat grin.

"Y'all want to sit in the car while I meet with Randall?" I wasn't sure how he'd take Ginger, or if she might say something inappropriate. I remembered my thoughts when I first saw her.

"Oh, no, we'll come with you," Honey offered. "I don't want to miss anything. You might need my professional opinion later on. Ginger might have some ideas, too." I wasn't sure what expertise Ginger might have that qualified her as an interior decorator. Especially judging by her fashion flair.

"Oh, I'd love to see the inside of the house. Come on, Honey, let's go!" Two against one. I shrugged and followed. I'd lost again.

An artist palette of spring flowers surrounded the cottage. Liriope, a.k.a. Monkey Grass, lined the walkway to the door. Azaleas dressed in pink, deep red, and purple lined the front of the house. On each side of the door stood large planters holding a variety of colorful annuals mixed with greenery. It looked like God had reached down and blessed this little piece of land, splashing color everywhere.

I startled when the door opened before I knocked. An older version of Johnny Depp stood in front of me. An image of Captain Jack Sparrow in *Pirates of the Caribbean* popped into my mind. I caught myself before I laughed out loud. I could tell the girls thought the same thing when their mouths dropped open.

"Hi, you must be Skye." Randall stuck out his hand. "I'm Randall Wade."

I shook his hand. "I'm Skye Southerland and this is my friend Honey and her cousin Ginger." He shook their hands and stood aside for us to enter.

"Come on in." I sized up the room immediately. I couldn't imagine what he wanted done. It looked great.

A floral imported area rug covered white oak floors. The room boasted sunshine yellow walls with white wainscot paneling. A padded window seat, flanked with floor to ceiling shelves, filled the front wall. Two white wing-backed chairs sat beside a teal green antiqued hutch with gold overlay. A teal coffee table stood sentinel in front of a white flowered couch with ottoman.

After a tour of the rest of the house, we sat in the charming living room and discussed the changes he wanted. New jobs always thrilled me. Ideas ran through my mind like wild horses. When we finished discussing the changes he asked questions about Sylvia and her death.

I decided to ask my own questions in return. "Did you know her long, Randall?"

"Actually, I drew up the plans for the tea room she intended to build in her front yard. She told me what she wanted," he lifted a shoulder, and his voice dropped a little. "It was her business what she wanted to do with her property. I have to admit, it made me wonder about her sanity."

"We've been acquaintances for years and she's always been a little unconventional." Not to mention downright ornery.

He stood up. "Well, she spoke highly of your work and I was pleased with what I saw. I look forward to you starting on my house. I'll give you an extra key and you can come and go as you please. I'm only here on some weekends." He strolled over to a small desk and took out a key.

As we walked out, he addressed Honey, and asked her for a private word. I figured he wanted to ask for a date, so I told her we'd wait in the car. Ginger and I made small talk about the visit.

When she returned, she wore a goofy grin. "What are you grinning about?"

"He asked me for a date. He's going to call me so we can set it up," Honey said.

"What is it with you two? Are you giving off some kind of secret vibes or maybe you just put a spell on these men?" I had to admit I was a little jealous Honey still had the ability to turn a man's head. The only head I ever turned belonged to Mitch. I knew in reality, that's all that really mattered though.

"What about *Robert?*"

"Oh, I haven't forgotten him. I'm just putting him on the back burner until we get this investigation solved. That's why we need to hurry."

"I thought we needed to hurry to keep us out of the caboose for a murder charge."

"Yeah, that too."

Ginger, riding shotgun, pointed her finger. "Honey, I'm jealous. You get to go out on a date and I don't. Are you sure I need to abstain from dating while I'm rehabbing?"

"Yep, we don't want to put temptation in your way," Honey replied.

"Hey, I've got a great idea. I'll go out with you and Johnny Depp. You don't want me staying home alone do you?" I heard her chuckle. "I just might get into some trouble."

# CHAPTER THIRTEEN

I heard a deep intake of breath. It looked like Honey had bit off more than she could chew.

"Uh, I'll think about it," Honey said.

Ginger performed a little dance in her seat. "Hey, can we go to one of those fancy places y'all eat at for supper?"

"Best idea I've heard all day," Honey said. "Why don't you call Mitch and see if he can meet us at Mary Mac's?"

"I'll do that. He's real busy at the store, but it sure wouldn't hurt him to take a break. Would you grab my phone Honey?" She reached in my new Lily Bloom bag and pulled out my phone.

"Here ya' go."

He jumped at the chance to get away from work for a while. We agreed to meet up in an hour. I looked forward to eating at Mary Mac's Tea Room even though the restaurant sat right downtown on Ponce de Leon Avenue. We'd have to fight the evening traffic, but the payoff was worth it.

Mary Mac's opened in 1945, and specialized in serving made-from-scratch down-home cooking. Many famous people have visited the southern style restaurant, leaving autographed photos for display.

"He said he'd meet us there." We hit gold and found a parking space right in front. The only drawback – I had to parallel park. It didn't take me but three tries.

"I wasn't sure you'd make it, Skye." Honey emitted a sigh of relief.

"Yeah, me either," Ginger concurred.

"Okay, okay. It took me a while, but I got the job done. Come on, let's go in and get a seat before the Capital crowd converges." Everyone knew the Governor and state employees enjoyed eating at the famous restaurant.

We sat in one of the six dining rooms and studied the menu while we waited on Mitch.

"Oh, look! They have pot likker and cracklin' cornbread. I have to have some." Ginger fairly drooled over the menu. I had to laugh, because I totally understood. Not so much drinking pot likker, the juice left from cooking greens, or even cornbread with pork rinds cooked in, but about the southern menu. I loved the fried green tomatoes and sweet potato soufflé. For dessert, the Georgia peach cobbler was to die for. I decided what I wanted and placed the menu on the table.

"Hey, what did y'all think of Randall?"

"Well, I think I'll find out more about him this weekend," Honey said.

"I kind of found it odd he kept asking questions about Sylvia's death. Maybe you can ask him some questions while y'all are out on your date, Honey."

"Oh, just like a spy," Ginger said.

Mitch arrived while we discussed Randall. I raised my hand and gave a little wave to catch his eye. He smiled, nodded in acknowledgment, and hurried across the room.

"Hi, Sweetie." He leaned down and kissed me lightly on the lips. A tingle traveled to the pit of my stomach.

He winked at Honey and Ginger. "Hello, ladies. How are y'all doing?"

Ginger smiled and said, "I'm doin' much better now that I know they serve pot likker and cracklin' cornbread."

Mitch threw back his head and laughed so loud it brought stares from the other customers.

"Mitch, have a seat darling." Mitch's voice had a way of carrying and he didn't even have a clue.

We were halfway through our meal when Honey dropped her fork with a clang. "Oh-my-goodness look who just walked in." Of course, we all gawked. "There's Jimmy Carter and Roselyn." Sure enough, the famous couple sat down at a table across the room.

"Who's that?" Ginger asked as if she'd never heard of them.

"You're kidding, right?" Honey shot her a look like she'd lost her ever-loving mind.

"Yeah, just kidding. He's the most famous governor Georgia's ever had." The rest of the meal passed with little conversation while everyone stuffed themselves with the best food in the south. By the time we finished eating, I wanted to go home and soak in a tub of hot water. I asked Honey to meet at the condo for breakfast and we'd discuss the list we'd made.

Honey and Ginger caught me in my pajamas when they arrived the next morning. "You mean you don't have on your new teddy?" Honey and Ginger roared.

"Very funny girls." I moved aside for them to enter. "Come on in. I have pound cake and I made some fruit compote to put on top."

"Yummy. I'm so hungry I could eat a squirrel," Ginger said.

"You're kidding, right Ginger?" I've eaten a lot of things, but squirrel wasn't one of them.

"Nope. Serious as a porcupine in love. Nothin's better than squirrel stew unless it's possum stew."

What in the world did they eat in the North Georgia Mountains? "Well, there's no squirrel here, just pound cake. Honey, why don't you pour us some coffee while I get the list?"

She poured three cups of steaming brew, and sat the coffee pot in the middle of the table. "Who should we talk to first?" She sipped the brew and made a face. "Hotter than a summer day in the south."

"Why don't we talk to John Abbot since he lives next door to Sylvia's? Honey didn't you say he was the one who discovered her body?"

"Yeah, he did and he said he saw somebody run off."

"What if he just said that?" Ginger took a break from her second helping of cake topped with fruit. "And he didn't really see anybody."

"That's a good question, Ginger. I hadn't thought of that. A ruse to cover his own tracks." I gathered the dirty dishes and headed to the kitchen. I suddenly remembered John knew Ginger from the club where she worked. A disaster in the making.

"Uh, Ginger, do you want to wait here while we visit John?" I crossed my fingers hoping she'd consent. No such luck.

"Oh, no, it won't bother me. I don't want to miss all the fun." She gathered her dishes.

"Won't it make you, uh, uncomfortable knowing John and all? His wife might be there, too." I wondered if Stephanie knew of her husband's hobby.

"Don't worry, Skye, I won't say anything. I promise."

"Well, let's quit jabbering and head on over there," Honey said. She grabbed the last piece of pound cake and took a big bite. "One for the road."

We didn't encounter any problems on the drive to John's. We pulled up to the gated driveway and rang the call button. After I announced myself, we were buzzed in. The winding driveway ended at a beautiful gray stucco three-story mansion.

"Wow-wee, look at that house. Is that a castle?" Ginger's green eyes grew big and round. "What does he do for a living?"

"He's a lawyer," Honey said. "And he's running for city councilman."

We parked in front of the house and strolled up the walkway. Azaleas of every color lined the rock walk. I didn't expect John to open the door. Why wasn't he working?

"Well, to what do I owe the pleasure of this visit?" He smiled until he noticed Ginger. His face looked like it'd stolen the white right off a gardenia from his front yard. I was afraid he'd hyperventilate.

"Hi, John," Ginger said. She gave him a wink. "I've seen your campaign posters around town, I hope you win the race." I saw the relief spread over his face as Stephanie walked up.

"Hi, Skye. Hi, Honey." She looked at Ginger. "And you are?"

"This is my cousin, Ginger."

Stephanie stuck out her hand. "Glad to meet you, Ginger."

Ginger took it and pumped vigorously. "Same here."

"Would you like some tea?" We looked at each other and shook our heads.

"We just ate." I explained. "As I said on the phone, we won't take much of your time, but we wondered if you were informed of the circumstances of Sylvia's death."

He indicated for us to sit and I chose an overstuffed rocker-recliner. I received quite a shock when I sat down and the rocker lurched back. When I placed my feet back on solid ground my breathing steadied to a normal rhythm.

John sat on the edge of his seat. "We've heard it's been ruled a homicide." Stephanie perched on the arm of his chair.

Before I answered, someone yelled, "Thought I saw some Yankees ride up! Let me at 'em."

*Good grief what in the world was that?* I looked around to see a little old man running toward us in polka-dotted boxers, brandishing a gun.

"Y'all Yankees?" he leveled the shotgun at us and sighted down the barrel.

# CHAPTER FOURTEEN

Honey shot out of her seat, placed her hands on her hips and stood her ground. "No sir, we surely aren't Yankees."

"Well, all right then, carry on!" He left the room as fast as he'd come in.

Stephanie's face changed red as Honey's lipstick, and John sputtered. "I'm so sorry about that. Uncle Jack has got some Alzheimer's issues. He can't get the Yankees off his mind." He offered us a sheepish grin. "Don't worry, it's not loaded."

I couldn't imagine leaving guns out with Uncle Jack around. "Oh good," I squeaked. We spotted him through a picture window patrolling the backyard.

"I've warned you about keeping your safe locked," Stephanie hissed, jumping up.

"I'm afraid that's my fault. I have a gun collection and sometimes when I'm cleaning my guns I leave the cabinet unlocked," John said. "I keep the ammo separate, where he can't reach it."

"I'll get it back from him." Stephanie followed the man into the backyard where he drew a bead on a squirrel. "Uncle Jack!"

While we watched her persuade him to surrender the weapon, I jumped in with both feet. "Honey said you discovered Sylvia's body?"

"Yes, it was early in the morning and I went outside to get the paper. It was barely light outside, but I saw somebody running from the house.

I ran over and found her lying on the floor and called 911. The EMTs said she'd died instantly." John shook his head.

Stephanie came back in carrying the gun over her arm. *Thank you God for small favors.*

"Sylvia wasn't very nice to you at the party," I said. "She told me she had no intention of voting for you and would make sure all her friends voted against you as well. Why did she feel so adamant?"

Honey piped up. "She was riled up like a nest of angry hornets."

"I'll tell you what she was angry about, it's no secret. I voted against her when she requested permits to build that monstrosity. Unbelievably, the council passed her request against my protest. I think she had some of them in her pocket if you know what I mean. Who ever heard of a Japanese teahouse on stilts? Sometimes I think she was plum crazy." John rolled his eyes.

"John's right. We didn't want that atrocity ruining our neighborhood," Stephanie offered. "I'm sorry she's gone, but really. Right honey?" Neither one of them appeared very sad about Sylvia.

"Were you aware of the teahouse?" John asked me.

"Yes, I knew about the Japanese teahouse she'd planned on building; she'd shown me the plans but I didn't think she'd follow through." Randall Wade had shown us the plans for the twenty foot tall tower. She wanted a place to invite her bridge partners with an unobstructed view of the neighborhood.

"Talk about your killer views," Ginger said.

"I have one more question to ask," I said when I found my tongue again. "Did you hear Honey's story about the old desk and a treasure map?" I heard a deep intake of breath from Honey. I sent her a look telling her to keep quiet. I hoped she'd figure it out.

"Well, I thought she spun a convincing tale. I really didn't give it a second thought. I suppose it's possible. I've heard of hidden compartments in antiques." I wondered how forthcoming he really was.

We talked a few more minutes before we said our good-byes. John's eyes registered relief when we announced we needed to go. Ginger had kept her promise to keep his dirty little secret.

We started talking all at once when we got back in the car. "What do you think? Did he do it?" Ginger had already made up her mind, "I think he's guilty. He was angry with Sylvia for building that teahouse of hers."

"You have a point, Ginger, but we haven't talked to any of the other people who were at the party."

"I've got an idea," she said. "I've got some contacts at The Silver Spur. We can go there tonight and ask questions. I'll be on my ole' stompin' grounds so maybe I can find out the word on the streets about Sylvia's murder."

"Oh, that's a great idea," Honey agreed. "We can dress up in Western clothes and act like we're there to have a good time. Like undercover cops."

I looked upwards. *Lord, please help me out of this mess.* I needed a break. "Why don't we stop and pick up some sandwiches and head over to Piedmont Park to eat? It's a beautiful day for a picnic."

Honey jumped on the idea. "That's great! I heard they're having a battle of the bands."

Ginger chimed in, "Any country bands playing? I just love Allen Jackson. Isn't he the cutest thing with that long blonde hair? Speaking of elected officials, did y'all know Allen's sister was once mayor of Cave Spring, Georgia?"

"I didn't, Ginger, but thank you for that bit of trivia. I have to admit he's good looking." I preferred classical music, but I listened to country enough to recognize some of the artists.

We stopped at Subway and ordered sandwiches to take with us. I happened to have an old quilt in back of the car. We gathered the quilt I used to transport furniture and our food and headed to find a spot in the crowded park. The music blared, so I suggested we sit as far away as possible.

If you ever want a day of people watching, go to Piedmont Park. Every size, shape, and color of human beings filled the park. I loved watching people having fun together. I looked around and noticed a young couple holding hands, a family with two little boys, and plenty of senior citizens.

We spread the blanket on the ground. The air smelled of freshly mown grass. With all the rain we'd had lately a blanket of lush green surrounded us.

"Isn't this great?" Honey unwrapped her foot long club and took a bite. "Ummm, dewicious." She talked with a mouthful of sandwich.

I'd opted for a six-inch veggie. We'd laid our lunch out when something landed, splat, right in the middle of the quilt. "Yuck, bird poopy!" Ginger said. She shook her hand toward the sky, "darn birds!"

"Oh, no. Y'all get up and we'll flip it." We gathered our food and turned the offensive quilt over.

My stomach churned, but hunger won and I continued to eat. It didn't faze the girls at all by the way they ate. Even though we'd decided to sit away from the stage, I had a throbbing headache from the loud music. Any closer and I might have had busted eardrums.

Ginger pointed to a group of senior citizens, "Look at those old people. I wonder what they're doing with those binoculars."

Honey chuckled, "It looks like they're bird watching. They have birding tours once a week and the public's invited. I might join them one day." Several noticed us staring and waved. We waved back. "Think we'll be doing that when we retire, Skye?"

"Don't know Honey, I don't like to think about retirement. I want to stay as active as I can."

"Yeah, me too."

We finished eating and settled back to listen to the music. I tumbled forward and bashed my face on the quilt. A sharp pain shot up my back, setting my shoulder blades on fire. I screamed like a teenager waiting for the Beatles to come on stage. Honey's voice sounded far way when I heard her yelling "help, help."

# CHAPTER FIFTEEN

"What happened?" I shook like a leaf in a fall wind.

"You're not going to believe it Skye. This young boy ran up, knocked you over and grabbed your purse. He took off running in that direction." She pointed toward the crowd. "Look, a couple of men from the birding group grabbed him."

Sure enough, an angry teenager struggled to get away from the men. Honey pulled her cell out and called 911. Within minutes the park police had arrived.

"Ma'am is this yours?" An officer held up my bag.

"It sure is." I grabbed it from the man, looked inside and took inventory. I breathed a sigh of relief when I saw my billfold intact. Ask any woman and she'll tell you her life's blood is inside her pocketbook. To have your purse stolen could mean a slow death.

The Atlanta police arrived and as they arrested him, the young man started yelling he'd been bribed. He looked at me. "I didn't want your ugly ole' bag anyway."

*Excuse me; are you talking about my Laurel Burch?*

He eyed the policeman. "This man came up to me and offered me twenty dollars to swipe her purse."

None of us believed him.

"That's a likely story," an officer said. "What did he look like?"

"I don't know," he whined, "just some old man. Kinda' your age I guess." This *old* man was probably in his late thirties early forties. "I remember the dude wore a suit."

The officer handed me a card. "Ma'am, we'll need you to come to the station and file a report."

"Okay, we can do that." My insides shook like Sam, Honey's dog, after she had a bath.

"Wow! That scared the bejeebers out of me!" Ginger hugged her waist and swung herself back and forth.

"Yeah, me too. I couldn't move. Time moved in slow motion." Honey folded the quilt while I threw away the trash. "Well, one good thing comes out of this. I get to see Robert again." She held the quilt under her arm while she fluffed her up hair.

"Too bad I've sworn off men for now or I'd give you a run for your money," Ginger said.

With Mitch in my life, I didn't have to worry about the dating game. I knew at the end of the day someone waited for me. In the evening we'd unwind and tell each other about our day. I knew Honey missed that in her life.

---

"Hi, Donna. Good to see you again." Donna's eyes opened wide as we walked in, disheveled and windblown, from the park. My ears still rang from the loud music and my back throbbed from the body blow I'd received in the mugging.

"You again? Are y'all here to see Detective Montaine?"

"Is he here?" Honey looked back toward his office.

"No. He's on a call." The phone rang and Donna stuck her finger in the air indicating she'd get with us in a minute. She finished in a shake of a lamb's tail. "What can I do for you?"

"We're here to file a report," I said. I handed her the officer's card.

"Yeah, some little twerp stole Skye's purse," Ginger offered.

"The one you're holding?" Donna looked skeptical. When I told her what happened, she walked over to a file cabinet. "Here ya' go." She handed me a form to fill out. "Please document the attending officer's name."

We sat in a row of folding chairs while I filled out the report. Honey and Ginger recounted the crime so I wouldn't forget any details. As I finished up, Detective Montaine came in.

"Well, hello!" He honed in on Honey. "What's going on?"

"Skye got her purse stolen at Piedmont Park. A kid said somebody paid him twenty dollars to steal it. The officers told her to come to the station to file charges. So here we are." For the first time he noticed me and Ginger.

He removed his hat and gave us a nod. "Hello, ladies. When you finish that why don't y'all come on back to my office?"

"Okay!" Honey spoke before I had a chance to answer.

I handed the clipboard back to Donna. "You know the way," she said and pointed to the back.

The detective looked up from his monitor and motioned for us to enter. "Have a seat. When did this take place?" He ran his hand through his hair.

"Just this afternoon," Honey said. She batted her eyes at the detective.

"I have a theory. I think the attempt to steal your purse is connected to the map. It's just too much of a coincidence." He shook his head.

We looked at each other. "Wow, I didn't think of that. If someone paid the kid to steal my purse it was premeditated?"

"That's right. You ladies need to be careful. It's likely more than one person's privy you had the map and they're still looking for it. I'm afraid your life might be in danger." His chair squeaked as he leaned back and put his hands behind his head.

"Hey, do you think it could have been John? Maybe we made him mad because we asked him all those questions." I coughed, and Honey nudged Ginger. Ginger's mouth was going to get us in trouble. "What?" Ginger shrugged. "Did I say something wrong?"

He scooted his chair around the desk, leaned forward, and placed his hands on his knees giving us his full attention. "What's this about asking questions? You haven't been asking questions about the investigation have you? Because not only would you be sticking your nose where it doesn't belong, it could be dangerous."

"We know these people," Honey said. "What would it hurt if we ask them a few questions? They might divulge information to us they wouldn't to you."

He shook his head. "No, I don't need your help. Thank you anyway."

His politeness didn't ring true. Facetious, yes. How were we going to get around this road block? I'd have to think of a way.

"Well, don't let me hear that you've been investigating on your own. In the meantime, be careful. Somebody out there has it in for you." He stood up, indicating this discussion had ended.

# CHAPTER SIXTEEN

**D**etective Hunky walked us to the door. Good grief, now Honey had me enamored with the tall, dark and handsome detective.

"I'll be in touch, ladies. Call me if you think of anything else that might be important."

When we were out of earshot, Ginger spoke first. "Do you think we have time to interview anyone else before supper?" I'd never seen her so excited. I believed she enjoyed this detecting business; she certainly didn't have any reservations about moving ahead.

I checked my cell to see the time. I had several hours before Mitch arrived home. Speaking of Mitch, my phone played "Redeemed" and his name popped up. "Hi, sweetheart," I said as we stepped outside.

"Hi, Skye. How ya' doing, babe? Have your nerves settled down?" If he only knew what we'd just experienced he might not let me out of his sight. I'd save that for another time.

"I'm holding up great. I was just thinking of you and wondered what you wanted to do about supper." I asked Mitch to hold on and told Honey and Ginger to go ahead to the car, I'd be there in a minute.

"That's why I called. I wanted to tell you not to wait supper on me. I've got a lot of work to do at the shop so I won't be home until late. How about getting Honey to spend the night, or at least stay until I get back, so you won't be by yourself."

"I'm sorry you can't be home, but yeah, I'll ask her to spend the night." *I'm sure her shadow would like to stay, also.*

I watched for traffic before I opened the car door. I didn't want to lose a door and surely didn't want to lose my life as cars whooshed past. Once safely inside, I told the girls what Mitch suggested.

"Sure! In fact," Ginger bounced to the edge of the back seat. "We can go to The Silver Spur without worrying about him asking questions. We'll have so much fun?" I had a feeling our definition of fun differed quite a bit.

"I already have my outfit in mind," Honey said. "It's smart to dress up so we blend in and the locals won't suspect we're working undercover."

Like a flash, I had a vision of us literally hiding under a sheet trying to listen to the customers. I laughed out loud.

"What's so funny?" Honey jabbed at my side.

"Ow! That's where the kid struck me." I rubbed at the bruised spot. "I was just thinking about us hiding under a sheet. Get it? Working under-cover!" Laughter floated throughout the car as we enjoyed a laugh-out-loud moment.

"It's still early," Honey said. "Do we have time to interview somebody else before we go?"

"I don't see why not." I suggested Raphael, Sylvia's hairdresser. "I believe he works at We're Hair For You."

Honey looked in the mirror. "I have a thought. My hair looks ter-rible. Why don't we treat ourselves to a makeover? It's a great way to get a do-over and ask questions at the same time."

Ginger squealed in my ear. "Oh! That sounds like fun, Honey. My pink's fading; I need to get it colored."

"I'll give them a call and see if Raphael can take one of us. Ginger, you and I might have to use another stylist while Skye does her detect-ing." She pulled out her cell and dialed 411 for the salon's number. "They said come on in," she announced when she'd finished the call. "Raphael can take Skye and they have two other stylists available at the same time."

On the way to We're Hair For You, we chatted about different styles we might want. They provided a parking lot behind the shop, so fortunately I didn't have to parallel park. I think Honey and Ginger were relieved, too.

The hair boutique, a pink stucco building, displayed a palm tree mural on the front wall. I expected to see pink flamingos among them. Gave me the feeling of being in Florida.

Pink stylist's stations, pink walls, and even pink hair dryers continued the colorful theme. Black customer chairs and accessories accented the shop. The color reminded me of Pepto-Bismol pink, which reminded me of Mama giving me the concoction for tummy aches.

A teenager with a bad case of acne and short spiked hair, stood behind the counter. She blew an award winning bubble until it popped, leaving goo on her face. She peeled it off and stuck it back in her mouth. "Can I help you?"

"I have a reservation with Raphael, and my friends also have reservations," I said.

She checked the computer. "Yeah, you're down. Come on back with me and someone will help you in a minute." She led us to a room lined with sinks.

We waited in pink and black chairs. Honey leaned over and stage-whispered, "get a perm."

"What?" I thought I heard her say perm. I received my last perm in my teens.

"Yeah, it'll take a long time to get a perm and you can ask lots of questions. It's perfect." A young lady came and directed me to one of the stations. While she washed my hair, the massaging movements almost put me to sleep. That is, until she ran the water so hot I thought I would come right off the chair. "Ouch!"

"Oh, I'm sorry. Was that too hot?"

"Yes!" She finished without scalding me again and showed me to Raphael's chair. Honey and Ginger were directed to their chairs, too.

Raphael's ensemble consisted of a burgundy silk shirt tucked into too tight jeans. He'd left open the top buttons of his shirt revealing a sprinkling of chest hair. His heels were so high I feared he might twist an ankle. His red hair nearly matched his shirt. I tried not to stare, but I failed. He reminded me of someone straight from the seventies.

While he dried my hair with a fluffy white towel, his eyes met mine in the mirror. "Well, what can I do for you?"

I surprised myself when I answered, "A perm."

He fingered my hair. "Humm, a perm. I haven't done one of those before, but I believe I can do it. Sugar, don't you worry about a thing, Raphael will fix you right up."

A red flag should have flown when he said this would be his first perm. I didn't listen to my gut and I paid for it. I've often wondered if that little gut feeling we get is God's way of telling us we'd better think twice before moving forward. Too many times I've ignored the internal warning and regretted it later. I'd look back on this as one of those times.

He stared at my reflection in the mirror. "Aren't you Sylvia's decorator? Or rather *was* her decorator." He stopped combing my hair and shook his head sadly.

"Yes, I attended her party. You were there, too, weren't you?" I knew he'd attended of course, but I wanted to hear his version.

"Of course, I went. I wouldn't have missed it for anything. Sylvia and I were like this." He crossed his fingers. "She named me in her will you know."

I didn't. Why in the world would she name her hair stylist in her will? For goodness sake, she had a daughter and grandchildren. He read my mind.

"She was mad at her daughter and son-in-law and changed it the week before she died. He hasn't approached me about it, so she probably didn't tell him. She changed it whenever she got mad, then she'd change it back. I guess she didn't have the opportunity to reverse it this time." He kind of shrugged and looked for perm papers in his drawer.

While he speed rolled my hair, he chatted freely. "That money will come in handy. Not afraid to tell you I can go ahead with my plans for expansion."

"You own this salon?"

"Yes, when I opened, I had no idea I'd become such a success."

Humph, time to change the subject. "By the way, did you hear the story my friend told about Blackbeard's map?" I wrinkled my nose at the stinky solution he doused on my hair.

"What a hoot."

"So, you don't think it's for real?"

"Of course not. I'm too smart to fall for something like a hidden treasure map. Do you?"

He blotted the solution running down my forehead and sat me under the dryer. He promised to check me in a few minutes.

The dryer noise whirled in my ear, and I sat alone with my thoughts. Being named in Sylvia's will guaranteed him top billing on our suspect list. He admitted he needed the money for his expansion project. I couldn't wait to tell the girls.

"Hey, Skye!" Honey's face materialized under the hood. "You asleep? Look, you have drool on your mouth."

"Oh!" I swiped at my mouth. Then I panicked. "Get Raphael!"

"All right. Calm down."

Calm down? I knew I'd been under the dryer too long. Where was he?

Raphael came running. "Oh, honey, I'm sorry. My architect and I were on the phone discussing my new addition. Time got away from me."

Raphael hurried me over to the sink and rinsed off the solution. He spun me away from the mirror and unrolled my hair. I sat on my hands while he blow-dried my hair. Then, he slowly eased the chair around.

"Oh – my – goodness!"

# CHAPTER SEVENTEEN

I didn't need my glasses to see curls upon curls covered my head.

Ginger summed it up quite well. "You look like a poodle."

Raphael had the nerve to placate me. "Don't worry, honey, Raphael can fix it for you." I had no intention of letting *Raphael* touch me again.

"No, thank you. I just want to go." I never thought I'd envy Ginger's pink-streaked hair. She looked cute, while I looked like I'd stuck my finger in an electric socket. To add insult to injury, I had to pay for the colossal disaster; at least Raphael had the class to give me ten percent off.

I started the car and high-tailed it out of the parking lot. Not that escaping would help anything. "Sorry about that, Skye. I never dreamed he'd leave you under too long," Honey said. She spoke so low I barely heard her.

"Aw, it don't look so bad, Skye. It'll grow out. Just think, it'll be easy to take care of." Ginger didn't sound too convincing.

We drove in silence. I think they were afraid to say anything for fear I'd burst out crying.

While I wondered what Mitch would say, Honey finally worked up the nerve to ask if I'd garnered any information. "Did Raphael spill his guts?"

"One thing I can say, he gave me enough evidence to confirm he had a motive for murder. Sylvia changed her will the week she died and made Raphael her beneficiary. He's already planned to use the money to expand his shop."

"He's definitely needs to move to the top of the list," Honey said.

Ginger had questions, too. "Did he say anything about the map?"

"Yes, he said he thought the story Honey told was just that – a story. If he killed Sylvia, I think he did it for the money."

"You're probably right," Honey said. "But that doesn't answer why you were attacked at the shop—"

"And mugged for your purse," Ginger said. We pondered these problems while we rode along, until Ginger spoke. "We'll figure this out. Honey and I'll go home, change our clothes and meet you at The Silver Spur."

Honey agreed. "I can't wait to wear my new boots. I've been dying for a chance to show them off."

I'd forgotten about going undercover. "Okay, you want to meet around seven?" I looked forward to finding a hat to wear. Tonight and forever.

"Sounds good," Honey said.

I knew I'd gained a little reprieve when I arrived home and didn't see Mitch's car. I dreaded the moment he saw my hair. I knew the encounter was inevitable, but I appreciated even a few hours delay. Maybe if I washed and smothered it in conditioner my hair wouldn't resemble corkscrews. Checking the clock, I discovered I had enough time for a quick nap. At least, for a short while, I could forget about the mess I'd gotten myself into.

The sound of a doorbell intruded on my dreams. I groggily removed myself from bed and stumbled downstairs. I opened the door and found two middle-aged cowgirls smiling at me.

Honey had on a brand new pair of jeans with a tomato red shirt. She wore a leather belt with an over-sized belt buckle. Her new beige cowboy boots were trimmed in blue and sported gold tips. She looked like she'd stepped out of a western wear catalog.

Ginger wore a little dress, and I do mean little. Honey definitely needed to commence an intervention on Ginger's clothes if she wanted a new image. Oh well, as Scarlett said, "Tomorrow is another day."

"You're not dressed!" Honey stood with hands on hips. "What have you been doing?"

"Sleeping." I yawned.

"I sorta' figured with that crease running down your face." She barged in and took my elbow.

"Don't worry, it won't take long for me to change." My stomach grumbled, emitting a noise akin to a growling bear.

Honey said something and Ginger laughed. "Let us know if you need any help with that..." she bit her lip and pointed at my head.

"Oh, good grief." I hurried upstairs and slipped on jeans paired with a white blouse. I didn't own cowboy boots, so I settled for black trouser boots. I forced myself to look in the mirror and my heart jumped. My hair lay flat as a pancake on the side I'd slept on, so I finger-combed it hoping it'd bounce back. It didn't. I had one flat side and one curly side. Not much I could do about it, the girls were waiting on me. I found one of Mitch's ball caps and tugged it down, but the curls only sprung out as if they were angry at me for corralling them.

"That's not so bad," Honey lied. "Kind of gives you a softer look."

"Well, come on. Let's get this show on the road. I could use some vittles." Ginger guffawed. "Get it? That's cowboy talk."

"I get it, Calamity Jane." If we didn't need to clear our names I would never go out looking this ridiculous, but I wanted to eat, so we headed for the car.

I'd underestimated the distance to the Silver Spur. It took us forty-five minutes to get there. With the parking lot packed, I squeezed between a little red pick-up, that'd seen better days, and a King Ranch Ford truck sporting dully wheels, hogging two spaces. I hadn't visited many bars, but this one looked like it came straight from a movie. I warily walked into a smoke-saturated room, filled with a rank smell that went back to the seventies.

The structure itself looked like a log-cabin. Memorabilia from a western set hung from the walls and decorated the dining room. Steer heads, bridles, saddles, ropes, and worn out boots authenticated the western theme. Red and white checkered tablecloths covered the tables topped with lamps made from old horse shoes. The clientele were as colorful as the decorations. The smell of burnt firewood lingered in the air.

I looked around; glad the girls were with me. Several men raised their hands and waved at us. Well, it wasn't really *us* they waved at – they greeted Ginger. Howdys were heard throughout the building.

Ginger leaned in, "See, I told you I knew a lot of people. I'm sure we'll get some information tonight."

I hoped I didn't learn more than I wanted to know. A tall, lean cowboy strolled over. "Hello, Ginger." He removed his hat. "Good to see ya.'"

"You, too George. This is my cousin, Honey, and her friend, Skye."

He shot us a smile and took just a little too long staring at my head. I saw the wheels turning. "Uh, what happened to your hair? That a new style or somethin'?"

"Oh, Skye just had a little misfortune. It'll grow out. Right, Skye?" Ginger's enthusiasm failed to extend to me.

"Yeah, right Ginger." I wanted to hide under a table. It'd take forever to grow out. I'd have to go crawling back to my hairdresser, Sue, and explain what happened. Like she'd believe me. I tugged the hat down tighter.

George gave Ginger an up-and-down look. "How about coming over to our table for a while?" He pointed to a table filled with men and women laughing and having a good time.

"Uh, sure. That is if it's all right with Honey and Skye." We waved Ginger on. We chose a table close to the one Ginger joined.

"How about let's order some grub," Honey said. "That's cowboy—"

"Speak. I know." We laughed until the waitress came over. I began to enjoy myself in spite of my hair fiasco.

The waitress, dressed in black pants with a white fringed shirt and black cowboy boots looked older than most of the other wait staff.

Wrinkles covered her face like crags in a mountain. Honey would probably refer to her as "older than dirt."

"Hi, I'm Maggie and I'll be taking your orders. What would you like to drink?" Both of us ordered sweet tea with lemon. A Southern staple.

"Oh, got me two teetotalers here." Her bright smile minimized her wrinkles. "I don't get too many in here that orders tea." Maggie placed the menus on the table. " I'll get your drinks and take your food order when I get back." She waved at some customers across the room.

"Look at this menu. Everything is meat – not many vegetables," I said.

"Well, we are in a western bar, and cowboys love their steaks." Honey pointed to a colorful picture on the menu. "Speaking of steaks, I think I'll take this ten ounce sirloin and a baked potato." Honey folded the menu and laid it back on the table. "With the works."

Like I said, I don't know where she puts it, but she managed to eat twice as much as me and still stayed slim. If only I could do the same. If I looked at a cookie or piece of cake I gained ten pounds.

"I'm going to get The Silver Spur Burger. It comes with the works and you can get fries or tater tots with it. Like I need fries."

"You only live once. Go ahead and enjoy some fries. Oh, here she comes."

Maggie brought out two iced teas in Mason jars, with lemon slices stuck on the rims, and placed them on the table.

"How long have you worked here?" Honey never met a stranger and loved to talk.

"Oh, I've only worked here for ten years, but I've waitressed for forty. Everybody keeps asking me when I'm going to retire, but I tell them I got no intention of retiring, I'm just going to keep on working till the good Lord calls me home. Or that scoundrel Bucky gets back and we go on that Ozark holiday he's always promised me." She grabbed a tablet from her back pocket and poised to write down our order. "Ladies, what cha' gonna' have?"

We placed our order and settled down to talk about the murder. Before we knew it she returned with our meals. "Thank you, Maggie."

"I'll come back around to check on y'all, but just wave if you need anything."

Honey dug into her steak like a dog after a bone. I could hardly bite into the super thick burger. I savored a burst of fire-grilled meat. We talked little while we savored our food. I'd just finished, wiped my mouth, and scooted my chair back a little from the table, when two guys came over and sat down at our table.

# CHAPTER EIGHTEEN

"**H**i, girls, I hope these seats weren't taken, because they are now." One very large guy laughed at his own joke. "My name's Tiny," this 6'6" three hundred pound giant pointed to his accomplice, "and this here's, Snake."

"Why Snake?" Honey asked.

He pulled up a sleeve, revealing a tattoo winding from his wrist to his shoulder. "It's a boa constrictor. That's why." He grinned, revealing a couple missing teeth.

"Uh, we weren't looking for dates. We're just here to have a little fun," Honey said. "But that's a very nice tat."

"See I told you," Snake winked at Tiny, "you're playing for the other team." Tiny slapped his hand on the table, and they started to get up.

Honey's tea spewed from her mouth. "Oh, no! You've got it all wrong. Skye's married and we're—"

"I'm not..." I stammered, then noticed him staring at my hair. "It was a mistake."

I gave Honey a swift kick, afraid she would give away the real reason we'd come to The Silver Spur. I didn't want to make them mad, so I compromised. "Look, if you want to sit here until we leave it won't be long."

"Well that's right nice of ya," Tiny said.

I wondered how much longer Ginger would need. I glanced at the table where she sat with her head close to George's. They were laughing and it looked like they were having a good time. I tried to snag her attention, but she didn't see me. I thought about going over and asking her, when Snake raised his voice loud enough for everyone to hear. "I'm telling you Justin Bieber's 'One Time' is his number one song." His face flushed and his eyes bulged.

"Well, I'm telling you it's not. His number one song is 'One Less Lonely Girl.'" Tiny pushed right up in Snake's face.

"You don't know what you're talking about."

"Oh, yeah? We'll see who knows what they're talking about!" He pushed Snake in the chest.

Snake took his beer bottle and whacked the container over Tiny's head. Then the fur flew. Several men jumped up and joined the battle. Bodies fell everywhere, including one landing face up on our table. It was time to get out of Dodge.

"Come on, Honey," I yelled. "Get Ginger and let's go before somebody gets hurt." Honey grabbed Ginger and we flew out the door. Just in time. I heard sirens in the distance. I didn't wait around to see if they targeted The Silver Spur.

We didn't stop until we were in the car and on our way. "Man, did you see that? I haven't seen anything that exciting in a while." Obviously, Honey's definition of fun differed from mine.

"Are you kidding? I was scared as a turkey in November."

"Aw, that's just another night at The Silver Spur," Ginger said.

"You mean this kind of thing happens all the time?"

"Well, I wouldn't say all the time, but it happens." Ginger wasn't too upset about the whole matter.

Honey turned around and faced Ginger. "The big question is, did you find out anything while you were there?"

"Not much. But George said there was some guy that came around asking if anybody would pull a hold-up for him. Nobody took him up on his offer. This proves the attempted robbery was planned. This guy knew you had the map and he wanted it bad enough to hire somebody to kill for it."

"That's not exactly new information, but it confirms that we were targeted because of the map," I said. What had we gotten into? What would happen if that person found out I had a copy of the map. Our life could depend on keeping it secret. "Girls, we can't let the fact that I have a copy of the map get out. It would put our lives in danger."

"Skye's right. We need to be real careful."

I looked forward to returning home. I'd experienced more excitement than I wanted these past few days. My clothes smelled like smoke. I couldn't wait to get them off and take a soak in the garden tub full of bubbles. I hoped Mitch wouldn't ask where we'd been. I wouldn't lie to him, but if he didn't inquire, I sure didn't plan on offering any information.

We said our good-byes, after the girls decided to go on home. We promised to meet early and discuss who we'd question tomorrow. I soaked in the tub until my skin wrinkled like a prune, and donned a pair of pajamas, relishing the silk against my skin.

The cool sheets soothed my tired body. Before I could count sheep, I zonked out. My slumber consisted of Justin Bieber riding a horse and trying to rope a steer, yelling, "I'm number one, I'm number one."

I awoke to somebody nibbling my neck. "Oh, hi hon. I'm sorry I didn't wait up. I was just too tired."

"Don't worry, Skye. I had to work later than I thought." He kissed me on the lips. After all these years his kisses still stirred warmth in me. He ran his hand through my hair as he kissed me.

He jerked back like he'd been bitten by a rattler. "What do you have on your head?"

# CHAPTER NINETEEN

He turned on the table lamp. "Oh!"

His reaction pierced my armor. Tears blurred my vision. "Oh, Mitch, it was awful. Just awful!" I reached over and hugged him for reassurance. I muttered into his shoulder, "He left me under the dryer too long."

He pulled me away from him a little. "I'm sorry, hon. It's not so bad once you get over the shock." His hand went to his mouth, probably trying to cover a smirk.

I knew he intended to sooth my spirits, but it didn't work. I sniffed and wiped my nose on my pajama sleeve. "I'm going to get it fixed." I couldn't wait to call Sue first thing in the morning. I'd have to endure her wrath, but if she could straighten my hair, I'd endure the consequences.

"Come here." Mitch gave me a hug and we spooned together, his nose buried in the back of my head. It took a while to get back to sleep. If my hot mess of hair had any benefit, it prevented him from asking about the rest of my evening. I went to sleep saying a prayer of blessings.

Morning came early. Bright sunshine burst through the curtains, and the birds announced dawn's arrival. I stretched and looked forward to the day, until I remembered my hair disaster. I tried to get out of bed quietly so not to wake Mitch. My efforts didn't work.

"Good morning," Mitch said. "Want me to fix us some breakfast?" Mitch did most of the cooking. He loved to cook and I didn't.

I tried to duck into the bathroom to fight with my hair before he could take a good long look. "No thanks. The girls and I are going to the Flying Biscuit. Wanna' come?"

"I would, but I'd better go back to the shop this morning. Since the robbery, I've decided to go ahead and do a thorough inventory. I've been swamped." He ran his hand through his already messed up hair.

"Okay, but I just wanted you to know you're welcome."

"I know – thank you." He kissed me on the cheek.

After I left a 911 call with Sue, I slipped on a pair of khaki capris and a blue tee shirt. I donned a pair of matching Yellow-Box flip-flops. I loved summer!

I called Honey and told her to come on over we'd go out to eat. She arrived in two shakes of a lamb's tail. Honey had no intention of missing a meal. We had a Flying Biscuit on Peachtree so it didn't take long to arrive. Honey and Ginger hurried out of the car while I took my time. I didn't want anyone to see my hair faux pas.

We followed the hostess to our table where she handed out menus. "Your waiter will be with you in a minute."

Honey hadn't even looked at her menu when she declared, "Don't need the menu. This is one of my favorite places to come for breakfast. I've memorized my favorites."

"Well, I haven't, so I'll have to take a look," I said. I grabbed a menu and wiped off the plastic where somebody had left greasy fingerprints. In a matter of minutes a young man stood beside our table. He barely looked old enough to shave.

"My name's Ricky. Can I take your order?" He set down two carafes. One decaf and one regular. I went right for the caffeinated.

"I'll take the Flying Biscuit Breakfast." It consisted of two eggs, sausage and grits and I anticipated eating every bite.

"I'll have the Piedmont Omelet and a side of pancakes with that. I'm a little hungry this morning." *A little hungry?* Honey had just ordered a huge omelet, sausage, grits and a side of pancakes. Ginger ordered the Southern Scramble consisting of eggs, turkey bacon, collard greens and grits. I pictured the staff rolling us out in a wheelbarrow.

"Okie, dokie, it'll be right out. In the meantime, I'll bring some of our famous biscuits and jelly." He took the menus and headed off with our order.

I leaned in, "All right girls, who do we question first?"

Honey dug in her purse and pulled out a piece of paper. "I've got the list right here. We've several to choose from – Amber Styles, Bernadette Jackson, Sylvia's assistant, Abigail Smith and her husband Raymond, she cooked for Sylvia and he drove, Joan and Will Newton, her daughter and son-in-law, her bridge partners Madeline Palmer, Gloria Habersham, and Elizabeth Herring. Wow, we'll be busier than a centipede at a toe countin' contest." Honey took a deep breath.

"I sure never knew I'd be in the middle of so much excitement when I came to stay with Honey. All this time I thought she lived a dull life compared to mine. I see I'm dead wrong," Ginger said. Honey and I looked at Ginger the same time. "What?"

"Be careful how you use the *dead* word." Honey poured herself a second cup of coffee. Normally hyper anyway, she'd be as nervous as a cat in a room full of rocking chairs.

"Pass me some of that. I could use a second cup." At least, we'd both be jumpy.

Ricky arrived with all the plates balanced on one big tray. I held my breath. I never understood how they accomplished this feat without dropping everything. The food looked delicious. For the next few minutes we ate in companionable silence. Only after we were sated did we discuss whom we were going to see.

"Why don't we go see Sylvia's daughter? Surely she has some tidbits to share." Ginger wiped her mouth, sat back, and patted her stomach. "I wonder if she's aware of Sylvia's latest change to her will."

"That's a great question. I hate to deliver bad news, but her reaction might give us some insight." I pushed my grits around on the plate contemplating whether to eat the last few bites. Already full, I debated if I wanted to step into miserable? I gazed at the grits and opted for miserable.

"I believe we are going to uncover more than one motive for murdering Sylvia. She sure knew how to stir the pot." Honey poured her third cup of coffee. *Lord help us, please.*

We paid the check and walked out into the sun, bright as diamonds, reflecting off the car chrome. I looked up and silently thanked God for another beautiful day.

I spotted a yellow note stuck under my windshield. I'd parallel parked, which is not unusual in downtown Atlanta.

"Look, somebody left you something, Skye." Honey reached over the hood and picked up the paper. "Uh, oh! A parking ticket."

I snatched the ticket from her. "Oh, no!" I glanced at the offensive piece of paper. Another parking ticket I could add to my collection. "I didn't need to start my day off with a parking ticket."

"Well, it could have been worse. They could have booted it."

"That's true. Come on, I'll just make the best of it. We don't have time for this." I shoved the ticket into my purse. I'd think about it later. "Honey, can you look up Joan Newton's address on your phone?" She had the address in a minute.

"She's in Vinings, not too far from where I live. We can probably make it in fifteen minutes."

"Should we call her?" Ginger rode shotgun.

"No, we don't want to give her a chance to leave. We'll surprise her," I said.

Joan's house mirrored the others in the Vinings' community. Three story stucco with a circular driveway. Landscaped beautifully, it sat on a slight hill. A red Mercedes sports coupe sat in the driveway, parked in front of the door. I pulled up behind it.

The doorbell played the first few notes of *The Blue Danube*. Joan opened the door and her eyes went wide. Was it my hair, or seeing three uninvited women in her doorway? Dressed in what looked like a brand new tennis outfit, she obviously had other plans.

"What do you want? I hope you're not here to interrogate me like you did John and Stephanie."

My mouth dropped open and I suspected Honey's and Ginger's did, too.

"What? You didn't think Stephanie would call me?" She struck a protective stance with her arms folded across her front.

"Look, we won't take but a few minutes of your time." I hoped I sounded non-confrontational. "We're actually trying to find out who killed your mother. Aren't you curious who the killer is?"

Honey put her foot in the doorway. "Yeah, you wouldn't want them to arrest the wrong person would you?"

Specifically us. Maybe she wouldn't catch on to the fact that Will had gained a place on our suspect list. She moved over and swept her arm towards the inside. "I only have a few minutes, I have a tennis date this morning."

Shades of chocolate brown, trimmed with white wainscoting on the lower half of the wall, accented the living room. Off-white carpet several inches thick covered the floor. Two off-white wing chairs flanked a brown leather couch. We opted to sit on the couch while Joan chose one of the chairs. I thought I recognized the stylings of a decorator from Atlanta I'd admired at a recent trade-show.

"What do you want from me?"

"Were you aware that your mother changed her will right before she died? She left her hairdresser, Raphael, an inheritance," Ginger blurted out.

I watched Joan's face change from pink to red quicker than a John McEnroe serve at Wimbledon.

# CHAPTER TWENTY

Open mouth and stick in foot. So much for subtlety, but I had to admit being blunt prevented Joan from masking her shock.

She popped up like a jack-in-the-box. "What are you talking about? She did no such thing!"

"We talked with Raphael yesterday and he said Sylvia changed it the week before she died. That she did this all the time when she became upset with you or Will," I explained. "Was Sylvia mad at you about something?"

"Humph! She stayed mad about something. I thought she embellished when she said she changed the will – she said it all the time." She sat down like a deflated balloon. "Are you sure about this?"

"Well, I didn't see the will, but Raphael said he planned to use the money to expand his shop. I assumed he saw the will."

"That's just like Mama to do something outrageous, like leave our money to her hairdresser." She studied me, and my hand flew to my curls. "We could've used that money. Mama knew Will had recently struggled in his business."

"Did you say Will's business wasn't doing too good?" Sounded like a motive to me. I wished I'd worn that ball cap again.

"Uh, well, just a bump in the road. He said business would pick up soon. You know the recession has had an effect on a lot of business owners."

Honey scooted forward on the couch. "Un, huh." She didn't sound too convinced.

Joan stared at me. I cringed. "Did you say Raphael did your hair?" Her lip curled into a smirk. One I would see often unless Sue called soon.

"Yes, I did."

"I'll make sure I never ask him to do mine."

Quickly, I directed the conversation away from me. I looked around. "Is Will here?"

"No." She didn't offer an explanation.

"Where is he?" Honey's large personality made up for what she lacked in size.

"For your information he's working." Joan stood, placed her hands on her hips and glared at Honey. "His investment business is located in Decatur." She headed out of the room. "I don't want to be late for my lesson, so y'all need to excuse me." Obviously, our cue to disappear.

Outside, Honey called for the front seat so Ginger hopped in back. "She appeared truly shocked about her mother leaving Raphael an inheritance. Then again, she said her mother did this all the time."

"Sounds like a mean ole lady if you ask me," Ginger said.

"You've got that right. Who would antagonize their children by changing the will back and forth all the time? Sounds like she used it to control them." I looked over my shoulder to see if I could change lanes. Cars zipped by and not one offered to let me in. I saw a small space between a Mini Cooper and a Ford Fusion so I took a chance and gunned it. The girls squealed in unison.

"Are you trying to kill us?" Honey, paler than a mimosa blossom, hung onto the handle above the passenger door.

"I'm sorry, but nobody would let me in so I did what I had to do. You take your life in your own hands when you drive in Atlanta. You know that. I'll tell you like you tell me all the time. Lighten up, Honey." I laughed, but Honey and Ginger didn't laugh with me. "Sorry, I'll try to be more careful."

"You're right about Joan, though. She seemed genuinely surprised.

What do you think about Will having financial troubles? Sounds like a motive for murder if you ask me." Did Will kill his mother-in-law for money? I'd heard of people killing for less. We'd definitely consider him a suspect.

"Yeah, people kill for a lot less than money and it sounds like he was desperate." Ginger voiced my sentiments exactly.

"Let's pay Mr. Newton a visit next. I think it's listed under Newton's Investments. Honey, got that cell phone handy? Can you look up the address?"

Honey excelled when it came to smart phones. "Sure. Hold on a minute." She spoke Newton's Investments into her phone. "Here it is – 1582 Trinity Place. Close to downtown Decatur."

"Okay, let's pay Will Newton a surprise visit." I turned the Highlander in Decatur's direction.

"Look, there's the Atlanta Botanical Gardens. Why don't we stop and go in? My treat. I could use a good long walk. While we're there we can check and see if there's any positions open Ginger might be interested in," Honey said.

Ginger clapped her hands. "Oh, that sounds fun. I love the gardens."

"You've been?" The words flew out of my mouth before I could stop them. Here I'd tried not to judge and I'd just stereotyped Ginger.

"Of course, I've been. An old boyfriend took me once. Why did you ask that?" Ginger leaned forward between me and Honey. "And let me tell you, I've seen flowers in the mountains just as pretty if not prettier than those at the gardens."

I coughed, trying to hide my embarrassment. "Sorry Ginger, I didn't mean to hurt your feelings."

"I know my job's looked down on, but I've tried to live independently. I see it wasn't the best choice for me, and I'm glad my cousin offered to help me." She squeezed Honey's arm.

"Well, I'm glad to help and I know Skye's happy for you, too. We're all in this together." I appreciated it when Honey changed the subject to take the heat off me. She talked about the displays at the gardens. Every year they changed the exhibitions. Honey explained this year they displayed giant mosaic pieces of art by Niki de Saint Phalle.

With the main parking lot full we had to use the parking deck and walk. It was well worth the hike. After we purchased tickets, we stopped in the gift shop. Displays of ceramic flowers, butterfly jewelry, and hand painted stationary tempted me. I wanted to make a purchase, but decided to wait until we left.

The entrance opened into a courtyard where a large water fountain claimed the attention of tourists. In the center of the fountain, a larger than life, multi-colored mosaic of a Rubenesque lady stood watch.

"That's what I call a woman!" The colorful statue made those few pounds I needed to lose trivial. If this woman proudly showed off her body, I should be proud of mine. Extra pounds and all.

"It's beautiful isn't it?" Ginger stood gazing at the artwork.

"Yeah, all women are beautiful regardless of their size. Even those who come in small packages." Honey laughed and we laughed with her.

"Hey, Skye! Why don't you stand on the fountain and I'll snap your picture?" Honey constantly took pictures with her phone and posted them on Facebook.

"Okay." The girls helped me up on the narrow ledge. I should have refused when I discovered my feet barely fit on the edge. But I didn't. "I'm ready!"

Honey positioned her phone. "Back up a little. I can't get all of you in the frame."

I backed up precariously, but water on the edge caused my foot to slip. I tried to regain my balance. Too late. I caught nothing but air as I flailed my arms. The last thing I heard before I hit the water was my own scream.

# CHAPTER TWENTY-ONE

I splashed around trying to sit up. I sputtered and spit when I surfaced. So much for getting up close and personal with the mosaic lady.

Honey and Ginger ran over, each of them grabbed an arm and heaved me up. Water dripped from my wet clothes. I took my frustration out on Honey. "Look what you made me do!" My dignity took a fatal blow.

"Look what *I* made you do? If I'm correct, *you're* the one who didn't look where they were stepping." Honey stood with her hands on her hips, full of indignation.

Ginger acted the role of peacemaker. "Okay, y'all, it wasn't anybody's fault. Accidents happen."

"You're right, Ginger, I guess I needed to blame somebody for my clumsiness."

Honey came over and put her arm around my wet shoulder. "I'm sorry this happened to you, Skye. Let's get you home and into some dry clothes." For a minute, I thought I saw a grin on her face. "You have to admit it was kinda' funny. You should have seen it when you fell. Your arms and legs were going different directions. Actually, I think I snapped a picture of it." She pulled out her phone and checked her photos. Sure enough, an image of me looking like something on *Funniest Home Videos*, glared out at me.

I couldn't help but giggle. I'd lost any taming I'd managed to accomplish on my hair. My choices were either laugh or cry, so I chose to laugh. Honey and Ginger joined in and soon people gathered round to look at the spectacle of us gasping for breath in between guffaws.

With what little dignity I had left I held my head high, and we marched past the crowd. Glad to reach my car, I hopped in.

"Honey, would you take the wheel please? I'm too wet to drive." I just wanted to sit down, close my eyes, and pray this disaster would go away. How much more could go wrong? First my hair debacle, followed by a tumble in the water. When looking back, I realized those incidents were minor compared to what lay in store.

Honey's voice disrupted my thoughts. "Sure. I'll be glad to drive. Why don't we pick up something for lunch, and eat at your place after you change?"

"Sounds good to me." I couldn't wait to get out of these wet, soggy clothes. We stopped at a Subway and ordered club sandwiches for everyone. After we arrived home, I took a quick shower and changed. When I returned to the kitchen the girls were already eating.

In no time, we had finished up and headed for Decatur. The traffic moved easily that early in the day, but the flow could change any minute.

"Look! There's his office building." His business was located in an old two-story mansion style home. The trend was for offices to use historic homes for their space. Remodeling old homes had boosted my decorating business. I'd remodel the dwellings for office use. I thought about the job we were to do for Randall Wade and wondered how I'd fit it into my schedule with everything that had happened. I never dreamed my life would change so drastically in a matter of days.

We entered the house and checked the directory. Second floor here we come. A blonde, buxom receptionist sat at a desk outside his door. "Hello, may I help you?"

"Yes, we'd like to speak with Will Newton," Honey said.

"Do you have an appointment?"

I noticed the door to his office slightly open. I pushed past Honey and Ginger. "No, we don't. But he'll see us." I stuck my head in the door to announce myself. He sat at his desk, lovingly turning a sword over and over. I'd seen that same look on the faces of young people in love.

He looked up and saw us. He took the sword and quickly shoved it under his desk. He stood up and walked around the desk. "Skye, Honey, what are you doing here?" He roughed up his already disheveled hair. He shut the door, walked back around his desk, and plopped down into his leather chair.

"We're talking with everyone that attended the party." I reached into my bag and withdrew a packet I'd meant to give to Joan. "I thought Joan might want these and I forgot to give them to her. They're photos I took while working at Sylvia's." He took the pictures and put them in a desk drawer. "I have them on a flash drive at the office if she wants extra copies."

"Detective Montaine is questioning all of us and we're trying to help him find Sylvia's killer." I loaded for bear and shot directly to the point. "Were you aware Sylvia left an inheritance to Raphael?" He didn't even flinch at the announcement. The least I expected – a raised brow.

"Sylvia threatened to change her will all the time. We're supposed to meet with the lawyer in the next day or two and we'll find out for sure. But I swear, I wouldn't put it past her to do something stupid like leaving our money to *that* hairdresser, Raphael."

"Your money?" Honey spoke my thoughts.

He had the decency to turn red. He stuttered and cleared his throat. "I mean Joan told me Sylvia planned to leave her some money. We – she was counting on it."

*I bet you were.*

"By the way, was that story about the map real? I noticed the desk missing from Sylvia's belongings, so I told Detective Montaine about it." So that's how the detective found out about the missing piece of furniture. Will told him.

"Of course it's real. And we have the map to prove it." Ginger blurted out the information I'd tried so hard to keep under cover. "Oops, I wasn't supposed to say that was I?" Ginger grimaced and sputtered.

"We don't really have it, we just have a copy. Detective Montaine has the original."

"Ginger!" She had to be a natural blonde. "What Ginger means, Will, is that we found an old piece of paper with some markings on it. It doesn't mean there's a real treasure. It could have been a joke somebody played."

"I could sure use the money from a treasure. Contact me if you want a partner," Will offered.

"Well, you don't need to worry about that. The only plans we have for the map is to exhibit it as an antique." I needed to cover up the fact we considered the map authentic. "Um, could you tell us where you went after the party the night of Sylvia's death?"

He quickly replaced the hundred watt smile with a look of scorn. "I'm afraid my location during that time is none of your business. The detective can ask me if he wants to know. This conversation is over." He opened his office door and stuck his head around the corner. "Becky, would you please show these ladies out. They're through here."

Becky's Cheshire cat grin indicated her pleasure at showing us the door. It didn't matter. I had what I'd come for.

"Well, she sure enjoyed giving us the boot," Honey said when we were back outside.

"That's okay, because I think we got what we came for. He was obviously uncomfortable talking about the inheritance. I think he planned on the money to help him out of his financial trouble."

# CHAPTER TWENTY-TWO

"I think you're right. If he thought they were going to inherit the money and use it to pay off his debt, he definitely had a motive." Honey and Ginger took turns riding in the front, and Ginger had dibs on the passenger seat.

"Look, I'm sorry I opened my big mouth back there. I was so excited about having the map I didn't think." Ginger sounded so contrite I couldn't help but forgive her. But now another person knew about the map and he also knew we had a copy. That didn't bode well for our safety.

I noticed a missed call from Sue, so I called her back to see if she could tame this poodle-do.

"Hey," I said, hand over the mouthpiece, "She can see me. Do y'all want to go next door and get a mani-pedi while you wait on me?"

"Sure. Yeah. That sounds like fun." My appetite kicked in after Sue's call.

"She said give her about thirty minutes. Want to stop at Java Monkey and get a coffee while we're in Decatur?" A unanimous "yes." We parked in the Decatur Square across the street. Maybe the day wouldn't be so bad after all.

I tried to visit this quaint little coffee shop anytime I stopped in the area. I opted for a hazelnut coffee, Honey ordered a double espresso, and Ginger went with a chocolate frappe. All of us bought a piece of sour cream pound cake. We wanted to sit outside and enjoy the slight breeze, but we purchased our drinks to go. We needed to get moving if we were going to make it to A Cut Above, where Sue promised to work me into her schedule. I switched to my prescription sunglasses while weaving in and out of the traffic in hopes of making it in time. I swung into the parking lot with two minutes to spare.

"Come on girls. Don't want to be late."

"Yeah, you're just in a hurry to get your hair fixed," Honey said.

"You've got that right!" I hurried ahead of the girls. I spotted Sue in the back, working on a client, and gave her a little wave. Rick, the young man behind the counter, eyed my hair a tad longer than necessary.

He cleared his throat. "Hello, Skye. Do you have an appointment?" I imagined behind his plastered on smile he thought, "Boy I hope you have an appointment."

"Uh, yes I do. Sue told me to come on in."

"Okay." Rick looked back at Sue. "She's just finishing up. You're her next customer." We sat down to wait.

Shortly, Sue walked over to the waiting area. "Oh, my. You're right. This just isn't you." She ran her fingers through my hair. "Humm, it's worse than I thought. We'll give you an intense conditioning treatment, afterwards I'll cut your hair. We'd talked about keeping it long, but you might have to start over."

"Don't worry about that. It's summer and I'll do anything to get this mess of frizz off." Would Mitch approve? Probably not. But he'd like it better than leaving it fried.

Sue asked Rick to wash my hair and put on the conditioner. Honey and Ginger went next door to The Tropical Isle for their manicures. Sue and I talked about everything from the weather to Sylvia's murder. After she cut my hair, she placed a little color around my face to brighten it up. By the time Sue rinsed me out the girls had returned. Sue blew my new style dry and turned me toward the mirror. My mouth dropped open. My hair looked so different! Yes, she cut it short, but the curls were straight and the blonde highlights brightened my face. I couldn't wait to show Mitch!

"Oh, Sue! You worked a miracle!" I gave Sue a big squeeze. "Thank you so much."

"You're welcome. But you have to promise to stay away from other stylists in the future." I didn't want to tell her we were working undercover. My face warmed, but I told her I promised. I floated over to Honey and Ginger who were in a deep conversation.

"Look, girls!" Their eyes widened. They stood and rushed to hug me.

"Oh, Skye, you're beautiful. Mitch is going to love it. Let me see the back."

I twirled around. "I sure hope so. He's not used to seeing me with a haircut this short. But I think he'll approve."

"It looks real good, Skye." Ginger shot me a smile.

"Thank's, Gin." *Thanks, Gin?* Had she grown on me this quick? "Let me see your nails." Honey held out her hands. "Teal?"

"Why not? It's summer and I wanted a fun color. I think it's cool." She held her hands in front of her and admired her new paint job.

Ginger showed me her hot pink nails. "Honey treated me since I'm not working. I hope to find a job soon though."

"Ginger, I've got this big job I'm doing for Randall Wade, why don't you help us out? That'll give you time to search for another position. I can even give you a reference."

Ginger's face lit up. "Are you serious?"

"I sure am." I shot her a smile. The look on Ginger's face was worth a thousand words as the old saying goes.

"Thank you, I'd love to work with y'all." She danced in place. "Honey, did you hear that?"

Honey laughed and gave Ginger a quick hug. "Of course, I did, I'm right here."

We decided to call it a night and Honey and Ginger went home. I wanted to surprise Mitch with a nice supper. I opted for steak, baked potatoes, salad and buttered rolls. Could I pull it off? I knew he intended to work late so I had plenty of time to shop and cook. I just needed to call him and find out for sure when he'd arrive home.

Seven o'clock came a lot faster than I imagined. I had just finished setting the table when I heard Mitch's car outside, and with a quick glance in the oven door at my new do, I trotted to the door to greet him.

# CHAPTER TWENTY-THREE

"ow! Your hair looks great, babe." He pulled me to him and gave me a long, lingering kiss. "Feel better?"

"I sure do. Sue worked wonders. She said most women have a horror story to tell about their hair. I guess I was lucky until now."

He shook his head. "I don't understand about women and their hair, but then again I'm not a woman." He sniffed the air. "Um, what smells so good?"

I grabbed his arm and pulled him toward the dining room. I'd set the candlelit table for two. "I made your favorite meal tonight. I wanted to show you how much I love and appreciate you. I don't tell you often enough." I loved Mitch, but my conscience had given me a little kick in the tush for not telling him about our investigating.

We spent the rest of the evening chatting and catching up, except the part about my snooping. I hoped we solved Sylvia's murder soon. I didn't like a black cloud hanging over me and Honey. I went to sleep thinking about our interviews the next day. I tossed and turned unable to settle down. Sometime during the wee hours, I reached over to shut off the annoying alarm clock. But discovered the incessant ring came from my phone. Mitch had already left for work, and the sun shone brightly.

I answered to a cheery, "Hey sleepyhead, how ya' doing this morning?"

I moaned. "Honey, why are you calling so early?" Mitch and I had stayed up late talking.

"Early? It's ten o'clock. Come on, we've got things to do. There's still a lot of names we need to cross off our list. And it wouldn't hurt to squeeze a little fun in between interviews."

"Okay, give me an hour." I hung up and searched for something to wear. I chose walking length shorts paired with a red tee. I jumped in the shower and let the water run over my face hoping it'd wake me up. It took only five minutes to blow dry my hair. I loved it! I slipped on my clothes and a pair of flip-flops. Before I went downstairs, I checked my hiding place for the copy of the map. Relief spread through me when I discover it right where I'd hid it.

I went downstairs and fixed a cup of coffee while I waited on Honey and Ginger. A couple pieces of toast and jelly would do for breakfast. Mitch didn't want to wake me, so he left a note. He'd planned on having another late night at the store. Honey arrived in exactly an hour. I answered the door and discovered two very perky women.

"Y'all want to come in for a cup of coffee?" They both nodded.

"Why not," Honey said, "it won't hurt to have a quick cup." Honey poured her own and one for Ginger.

Honey blew her coffee and gingerly took a sip. "Umm, this is good." She set the cup down on the marble counter. "What should we do first? Something fun or interview somebody, or a little of both?"

"Let's do an interview and then take a break. I wondered if y'all wanted to go to the Aquarium. I read they're hiring and thought Ginger could check it out."

Ginger clapped her hands. "I'd love to go. I've wanted to visit the Aquarium. This could be just the job for me."

"Sounds good. My last visit was over a couple of years ago. Did you know you can swim with the beluga whales? Sounds like fun to me," Honey said.

"Why don't I call and make reservations?" Mitch wouldn't believe this. Then again, it wasn't our first time for a last minute adventure. Since

Honey came to work with me, she'd tried her best to show me spontaneity by example.

We were in luck. The receptionist said someone cancelled and we could fill the slot. The excitement was palpable.

"Who should we visit today?"

"The list is in the car, but I've practically memorized it," Honey said. "I think I can tell you who we haven't talked to yet." She grabbed a paper towel and pen to write down names. She shoved it toward me. I read the names: Amber Styles, Bernadette Jackson, Abigail and Raymond Smith, and the three bridge partners Madeline Palmer, Elizabeth Herring, and Gloria Habersham.

"Let's talk to Bernadette Jackson, Sylvia's assistant. She should have the inside scoop on Sylvia." I'd met Bernadette while decorating Sylvia's house. She also helped serve at the party.

"Okay, do you know where she lives?" Honey poured her second cup of coffee.

"She said she didn't live far from Sylvia in the Greenbrier Apartments. We can find her apartment number when we get there."

"I'm ready when y'all are. I can't wait to swim with the whales." Ginger placed her cup in the sink, grabbed her shoulder bag and headed toward the door. "Come on!"

I unplugged the coffee, switched off the lights and headed out. "We can take the Highlander." I slapped Honey's car. "Have you thought about trading in your Crossfire?"

"Nope, sure haven't. I love my Crossfire and usually two seats are just right."

I knew she had no intention of trading it, but I loved to tease her. "Hey, you want to drive. I wouldn't mind taking the passenger seat." I needed a break from fighting Atlanta traffic.

"Sure. Hand me the keys." Honey asked for directions to Greenbrier Apartment's. I discovered we were only ten minutes from Sylvia's. "Should we call ahead or wait?"

"Well, we don't have her number so let's just wait and see if we can catch her at home." Encountering light traffic, we scooted right over to Bernadette's. "Scroll through the directory and see if you can find her name."

"Here it is," Honey said. When Bernadette answered, Honey informed her we needed to talk to her about Sylvia's murder. It must have piqued her interest because she buzzed us right in.

She greeted us dressed in a watermelon colored sweat suit, hair mussed and no make-up. Dressed for a day in. "Thank you for seeing us on such short notice."

"Honey said you wanted to talk about Sylvia." The charming living room invited the stranger to come sit a spell. A teal green over-stuffed loveseat divided the living room from the dining area. Two beige recliners flanked the loveseat.

"As you know, everyone at the party is being questioned about her death. Detective Montaine indicated Honey and I are at the top of the suspect list. We decided to take the bull by the horns and ask questions ourselves. Maybe we'd find something the police missed."

"I will try my best to help."

"Tell us about Sylvia. Was she as eccentric as people claimed?" Honey scooted forward on the loveseat as if she didn't want to miss a word.

"I owed a lot to Sylvia. When I moved here from Jamaica, Sylvia gave me a job when I could not find one. She gave me a chance when no one else would. I was indebted to her. Sure, she was exactly like everyone said, obnoxious, opinionated, and judgmental, but for some reason she chose to help me. Oh, and eccentric, as you can tell by the tower she started in her yard. She had a dream of putting a tea house on top of it. No matter she would not be able to climb to it."

Tears streaked Bernadette's cheeks. She genuinely missed Sylvia. I reached in my purse, pulled out a Kleenex and handed it to her. A screech from the bedroom caused me and the girls to jump. "What was that," we chorused.

I couldn't figure out why Bernadette laughed while a woman died right in the next room. "Oh, that's just Tippy, Sylvia's cockatoo. She loved birds and Tippy is the only one left out of three. The other two had already died, so I brought her home with me. She can make a lot of noise when she wants attention."

"She sure got ours." Honey still looked a little pale. "Why do you think somebody'd want to kill Sylvia?"

# CHAPTER TWENTY-FOUR

"That is a good question, but a hard one to answer. She made enemies like most people make friends. It could have been anyone from the party. There wasn't a person there she had not embarrassed or upset. I am not sure about you and Honey, but if she did not she would have in time. She was just excited because you had finished the project and she was really pleased with it. Give her another week or two and she would have called you to complain." She shook her head.

Honey leaned forward. "Bernadette, what did you think of my story the other night about the pirate's treasure map?"

"You are a good storyteller. It is not unusual where I come from to hear stories about pirates and buried treasure. I have heard them since my childhood." Tippy continued to squawk, so Bernadette shut the bedroom door. "Would you like something to drink?"

I checked my phone. Nearly one o'clock. "Thanks, but we can't stay long."

"Speak for yourself, Skye. I'll have something, thank you."

Bernadette returned from the kitchen with three glasses of sweet tea. "I thought you might like some, too." She handed me a glass and I happily accepted the cold drink. "One strange thing about that desk though. When I went back to Sylvia's, I missed it. I mentioned it to Detective Montaine, but he didn't elaborate on it. I wonder if the murderer stole it."

Honey and I eyed each other. Why had I ever let her talk me into going to Sylvia's to get the desk?

"We've kept you long enough." I tipped my glass back to finish the last drops. "I really appreciate you letting us come by unannounced. We have an appointment, so we'd better hurry."

"Once again, thank you, Bernadette," Honey gathered the glasses and took them into the kitchen.

I liked her. She seemed genuinely upset about Sylvia's death. But maybe she'd endured Sylvia's mean spiritedness long enough and decided to kill her. I just didn't get that feeling, though.

Back in the car, Ginger leaned forward. "What time's our reservation?"

"We're supposed to arrive between two and two-thirty. If we're going to get there in time you need to step on it, Honey." Not that she needed prompting to drive fast. She usually drove like a NASCAR driver striving to keep the lead. She wove in and out of traffic until we exited off I-75 at Exit 249C and hit bumper to bumper traffic.

"Why did they put the aquarium right downtown on Baker Street?" Honey drummed her fingers on the steering wheel.

By the time we checked in and reached our floor we didn't have a minute to waste.

"Hi ladies, glad you could join us. First, you'll get dressed in wetsuits and meet back here where we'll go over instructions." Let me tell you, it wasn't easy pulling up those wetsuits. The task rivaled putting on a too-tight pair of Spanx. I glanced at Honey doing an Indian dance, hopping from one leg to the other, trying to get the rubber outfit on. We wound up helping each other.

We met up with another couple from Canada who'd come just for the experience of being with the whales. The instructors, Lindy and Brandy, went over the guidelines and showed us to a small tank where stairs descended into the water.

"Let's get in the water and meet the whales first," Lindy said. The cool water took my breath away. It didn't bother the girls because they jumped right in. "Okay, let's get familiar with the whales by rubbing their backs." I gingerly touched their silky skin. For twenty minutes we stood knee deep in the water bonding with the mammals. The time passed too quickly before we had to get out.

Honey poked me with her elbow. "Where's Ginger?"

"I don't know. She was here a few minutes ago," I said.

Suddenly, Lindy and Brandy were running over to another employee, and we heard one of them say, "No way! You're kidding!"

"What is it?" Honey and I followed them through a door that led into the main theater where a jumbo window allowed tourists to see a myriad of fish.

Honey grabbed me. "Who in their right mind would swim in this tank?"

"Oh – my – goodness! Look who it is!" Brandy pointed.

It hit me like a heart attack. "Are you kidding?" We ran to the window and sure enough, we saw Ginger swimming with the fish. Everyone, including us, tried to get her attention. I jumped up and down. Ginger must have thought we were waving hello, because she swam over to the window with a colossal smile on her face and gave us a big wave in return. The crowd clapped and waved back.

*Dear Lord please deliver me. Quick!* I've never liked attention. I would go out of my way *not* to draw attention to myself. Honey jumped right along with me, but Ginger just waved. Suddenly, I saw Lindy in the tank with Ginger. She grabbed Ginger's arm and pointed upward. They both swam toward the top of the tank.

With my focus on Ginger, I forgot I still had on my wetsuit. We stood in front of a roomful of people with their full attention on us. I offered them a little princess wave and ushered Honey into the back room. Ginger came out of the water with Lindy on one side and Brandy on the other.

"Wow! Did y'all see me? Wasn't that the most wonderful experience?" She ran and gave me a hug. "Thank you so much, Skye. I'll never forget this."

I knew I'd never forget it either.

Honey stood ramrod straight. "What were you thinking, Ginger?"

"Well, you said we were going to swim with the whales. I just started swimming and ended up in the big tank. I had no idea we'd be allowed to do that." She shot Honey a look of contrition.

Lindy and Brandy came over. "You weren't supposed to swim in the large tank. I think you've had enough for today. Please take your suits off and leave them in the changing room."

By the time we dressed, I just wanted to make a quick getaway. "Come on girls, let's get something to eat and maybe squeeze in another visit."

Since we were downtown, we decided to eat at the infamous Varsity. It's an unforgettable experience to hear the waiters yell out your order when ready. The Varsity originally opened in 1928, and is still going strong. Many famous people have eaten there over the years. I ordered a slaw dog with fries and the girls ordered hamburgers with onion rings. We shared the fries and rings.

I had to admit, after I satisfied my appetite with a healthy dose of grease, I felt better. The restaurant noise prevented us from hearing, so we waited until we were back in the car to discuss who our next victim – I mean *interviewee* would be.

"How about Madeline Palmer? She's one of Sylvia's bridge partners. I understand the group has played together for years." I wondered how they had stayed together with Sylvia's reputation.

"I have her address. We're on the same committee at church. I'll call and see if she's available," Honey offered.

I glanced in the rearview while Honey called. Ginger's head lolled back against the seat and her mouth hung wide open. I guess her escapade wore her out.

Honey disconnected her phone and returned it to her purse. "She said she could give us a few minutes. She has plans for later."

"I think we wore your cousin out." I pointed toward the back seat.

Honey looked in her visor mirror. "Haven't seen her that quiet since she's come to stay with me."

"At least she can't get into any trouble while she's asleep." At least, I hoped not.

Our laughter woke Ginger. "What's so funny?"

# CHAPTER TWENTY-FIVE

"**S**orry. Go back to sleep. We'll wake you up when we get to our next stop." Honey shot me a grin. Ginger complied, and continued snoring.

Beautifully landscaped, Madeline's ranch style brick home, sat in a cul-de-sac. Splashes of color surrounded the house. Pink and white Dogwood trees dotted the lawn. Honeysuckle and privet hedge assaulted my nose as we walked to her front door.

An attractive older lady answered the door. Dressed for an evening out, she wore beige pants paired with a white blouse and high heels.

"Hello, Honey. Come on in." She moved back so we could enter. "Who do you have with you?"

"Hi, Madeline. This is Skye Southerland, you met her at the party, and this is my cousin Ginger."

Madeline stuck out her hand. "Yes, I remember Skye from the party and I've seen her at church. Nice to meet you Ginger." We shook hands and took a seat in the living room. "How can I help you ladies?"

Honey took the lead this time. "I guess Detective Montaine's questioned you about Sylvia's death?" She continued when Madeline nodded. "Well, he's suggested that Skye and I are at the top of the suspect list. The truth is we're trying to keep ourselves out of jail. We thought you might have some information we could use to clear our names."

"Well, it seems to me everybody who attended the party is a suspect. How can I help?"

"Just tell us about your bridge club meetings and how y'all got along with Sylvia," I said. Laughter rang from behind us. A distinguished, older gentleman stood in the doorway.

"Oh, James, come sit with us." Madeline scooted over on the couch and patted the seat next to her. "Ladies, this is my husband, James." She gestured towards us. "You know Honey, and this is Skye, Mitch Southerland's wife, and this is Ginger, Honey's cousin." We shook hands.

"I couldn't help but overhear part of your conversation," James said. "Why don't you tell them about the time you threatened to kill Sylvia."

I couldn't help gasping, and Honey and Ginger sat up straight.

"James!" Madeline turned a shade paler than biscuit flour.

"Well, it's the truth. Madeline thought Sylvia and I were having an affair. She just about divorced me and swore up and down Sylvia wouldn't get away with it." James slapped his leg and doubled over in laughter.

"James, it's not funny."

"Anyway," he went on despite his wife's obvious displeasure, "Madeline went over to confront Sylvia. We finally had to come clean and tell her Sylvia had helped me plan a surprise party for Maddie. I tell you, it took a long time before the two would talk to each other again. I sure learned my lesson." He kissed Madeline on the cheek and poked her in the arm. Madeline didn't laugh.

"Well, I'm still not convinced she didn't have her eye on you James Palmer. I wouldn't have put it past her. She didn't care who she hurt, just so she got her way." Madeline glared at us. "Well, I guess you got more information than you bargained for."

"We've got plenty," Honey said. I raised my eyebrows at her hoping she'd take the hint to be quiet. I didn't want Madeline to clam up. "Skye, are you all right? You're making funny faces."

Their confession made me think we might get somewhere since these two knew Sylvia on a more casual basis. "What about the other ladies? How did she get along with them?"

"Well, there's Elizabeth Herring and Gloria Habersham. Elizabeth has been a partner for many years, but Gloria only a couple. She's the youngster of the group; she turned sixty-two this past February," Gloria smiled. If you're eighty I guess sixty's young.

"Did they have any grievances?" Our investigation indicated Sylvia made everybody in her inner circle mad at one time or another.

"Well, Elizabeth and Sylvia were always arguing about something or another. They could never agree on anything. You'd have to ask Elizabeth about that though. And Gloria just rubbed Sylvia the wrong way. She couldn't do anything to please her. Probably jealous."

She patted James's arm. "I guess we'd better go or we'll be late." She turned toward us. "I'm sorry we have to rush off, we have reservations."

"Thank you for your time," I said and stood.

"Yeah, you helped us a lot." Honey grabbed her sweater and purse.

James and Madeline walked us to the door. "Good luck clearing your names," Madeline said. They walked out with us and got into their car. I backed out. They followed and passed us.

"I guess they were in a hurry," Ginger said. "We didn't learn much from them."

"No, but Madeline didn't hide her feelings towards Sylvia. I don't think she liked her too much.

"Yeah, but did she hate her enough to murder her?" Honey handed me my phone when it played "Redeemed." I hesitated when I didn't recognize the number, but decided to answer it.

"Hello?"

"Hello, Ms. Southerland. This is Detective Montaine and I wondered if you and Honey could come down to the office as soon as possible?"

# CHAPTER TWENTY-SIX

"**O**f course. We're on our way." I hung up. What in the world did he want? To arrest us? *Oh, well, at least my hair will look good for the mug shot.* This past week had played havoc with my sensibilities. I feared I'd wind up in the home for the bewildered before this investigation ended.

I handed the phone back to Honey. "Detective Hunky wants us to come down to the station. He didn't say why. I noticed he called me *Ms. Southerland* and he called you Honey." I had to laugh at Honey's ability to attract single men. They say blondes have more fun. Honey and Ginger were out to prove this saying true.

"Wow, wonder what he wants. Doesn't sound good," Ginger noted.

"No, it doesn't, but I don't mind another opportunity to see Robert again. Maybe when all of this is over we can become an item." Honey released a huge sigh. "That's why we need to get this mystery solved. I can't picture Robert dating a jailbird."

I thought about calling the attorney Mitch suggested, but decided to wait until we found out what the detective wanted with us.

"I'm so ready to get this over with." We debated why he might want to see us on the way to his office. We seated ourselves in the hard orange chairs in the waiting room. I wondered who'd sat in these chairs and what cooties they'd left behind.

"I suppose you're here to see Detective Montaine." Donna acted like she perpetually sucked on a lemon.

Honey stood and walked over to the desk. "That's right. Robert called and asked us to come in."

"Humph!" She disappeared down the hall. A surly Donna returned in a minute and directed her comment to Honey. "*Robert* will see you now. You know where his office is." With that she plopped in her desk chair and dismissed us by returning to work.

Detective Montaine stood when we entered. "Hi there." He smiled at Honey and nodded to me and Ginger. "I guess you're wondering why I wanted you to come in." We nodded in unison. "I've received a couple of complaints this morning that you three are going around asking questions about the Landmark murder. Am I correct?"

Nobody answered. We looked at each other, waiting on somebody to take the lead. Finally, Honey answered. "Yeah, we have asked a few questions to some of the people that were at the party." She gave him a winning smile. "We're just trying to help you." She actually whimpered and batted her eyes.

It must have worked because he went easy on us. "I know you're worried about being suspects and you want to hurry the investigation along, but these things take time. And my main concern is that delving into murders could lead to big trouble. I wouldn't want anything to happen to you ladies." He looked directly at Honey. "I can't tell you not to talk to anyone, but I can warn you. How about sharing with me anything you find helpful?"

"We can do that," I said. We told him what we'd learned so far and he took some notes, cautioning us once again when we stood to go. He shook our hands, lingering a little longer with Honey. I thought he shook our hands so he could really hold Honey's.

The interview went better than I thought. He didn't say we couldn't ask questions so that meant we had the go ahead with our own investigation. I wondered if the time had come to tell Mitch. We headed down the road with no destination in mind. "Hey, it's about time for supper. Where do y'all want to go?"

"Let's go back to that cute place – I think it's Vinings Inn?"

Honey and I exchanged looks. "Uh, I don't think I want to go there tonight." *Or any other night for that matter.* "How about you, Honey?"

"No, no I don't think I do." Thank goodness Honey backed me up.

"Aw, that's too bad. I thought that was a right nice place. I have to admit I was disappointed they didn't have possum stew. Do y'all know of any places that have possum stew?" We didn't.

"I have an idea," Honey said. "Let's go to a Braves game. We can eat hot dogs while we're there. Ginger, you can pick up an application."

Ginger bounced up and down in the back seat. "Oh, yeah, let's go. I've never met a hot dog I didn't like."

I hesitated, not wanting an instant replay of the aquarium disaster. Then I thought, *why not?* I could get used to this spur of the moment thing. "Sure, let's do it!" We weren't that far from the stadium. The game day traffic going into the parking lot moved slowly. We took extra effort to note where we'd parked so we could find our car after the game. We parked under a purple hippo. Because we bought tickets at the gate, we acquired seats behind the outfield.

"Wow, the players look like ants from here," Ginger noted. Good thing they had the Jumbotrons. People surrounded us as the stadium began filling up. There were families with children, couples, and a Boy Scout troop. A couple of burley guys sat in front of us. They looked like they'd ridden in on Harleys. One sported long hair and a long beard reminding me of Jase on *Duck Dynasty*. The other one had a long braid and a scraggly beard.

We ordered loaded dogs and Cokes from the vendor. We settled down to watch the game. The Braves played the Cincinnati Reds. Our team finished their first inning with no runs. Next, the Reds were up with bases loaded. There were two outs and the batter had two strikes. The batter swung, the ball made contact, and I heard a loud crack as the ball came flying our way. It came closer and closer until Honey jumped up, closed her eyes and held out her arm. The ball plopped right into her palm.

We clapped and yelled at the top of our lungs. Ginger yelled "way to go Reds." Everyone stared at her including our burly seatmates. I wanted to crawl under my seat. "Ginger, why are you rooting for the Reds?"

"Oh, just wanted to add some spice to the game." She laughed and continued to root for our opponents.

Not only had she added spice to the game, she'd added spice to my life over the past few days. Even though she'd come close to triggering a heart attack several times, clearly she enjoyed living her life to the fullest. I'd always worried what other people thought, keeping me from being real.

Could Ginger teach me one of life's lessons? Watching her had definitely opened my mind to new possibilities. I needed to give myself a break and remember God didn't expect us to be perfect. I felt bad for judging Ginger without really knowing her and considering her desire to please God.

The game continued with the score tied at four; bottom of the sixth. Between innings, images of the fans flashed on the screen. They'd jump up and down, smile, kiss, or just offer a wave to the crowd. I enjoyed watching their surprise. Suddenly, I saw Ginger's image on the Jumbotron. A gargantuan smile adorned her face. She jumped up and waved vigorously.

I guess she forgot she was eating her third loaded dog with fries. Bubba and Rebel (the names I'd given the two biker fellows) leaped up, ketchup and pickle relish running down their backs.

# CHAPTER TWENTY-SEVEN

Their expressions belied their feelings. Bubba actually growled. She was so busy gaping at herself on the screen, Ginger didn't even notice. I offered Bubba some napkins, but he knocked my hand away.

"I'm so sorry. She didn't mean to dump her food on you." He looked at me like I'd grown another head.

Ginger suddenly realized what she'd done. "Oh, no! Did I do that? Here let me help."

They gazed at Ginger as if seeing her for the first time, eyed her shorts and tee-shirt and their demeanor changed. Rebel actually smiled, "Sure, you can help me anytime, doll."

She handed them a wad of napkins and helped him dab at her mess.

"How about writing down your number on this napkin for me?"

She wrote down her number and handed the napkin back to Rebel. "I'm involved in a project now. But in a couple of months I should have some free time."

Bubba asked Honey for her number as well, but she demurred explaining her involvement with someone. I assumed she meant Detective Montaine.

Honey and Ginger possessed the uncanny ability to draw men like bees drawn to honey. Not that I was interested in attracting men, but when you hit middle age it's nice to know you can still turn a head or two. I reminded myself, all that really mattered was if I could still turn Mitch's head.

We ended the evening on a high note. The Braves won nine to four. The traffic leaving the stadium drove bumper to bumper. Fortunately, I was familiar with the area.

I called Mitch and informed him we were on the way home. He said he was on his way home, too. I looked forward to inventory ending so he could get home earlier in the evening. He'd been concerned about the store ever since the break-in. I missed his company, and I couldn't wait until someone solved Sylvia's murder. I enjoyed hanging with Honey and Ginger, but their companionship wasn't the same as having Mitch around.

I told the girls I needed to go to Lake Lanier tomorrow and take some measurements at the Wade cottage and I'd like for them to go with me. So we planned to meet in the morning. I invited Ginger and Honey to come in; when she announced the ladies room called.

I strained to see the door knob in the dim light. When I tried to insert the key, the door squeaked opened. I flipped on the outside light. I immediately noticed gouges on the doorframe. "Look! Somebody's broke in!"

"Don't go in, Skye. They might be in there. I think we need to call Robert," Honey noted.

"She's right, Skye. Let's wait."

Even though my instinct said hurry and enter so I could find out the damage to the house, I decided they were right. I called 911, and we waited in the car. In less than ten minutes two squad cars pulled up. Officers Vicki McCluskey and Sonny Day came over to introduce themselves and find out our concerns. They told us to wait in the car while they checked out the condo. While they were inside another car sped up. Detective Montaine jumped out of the car and hurried over to us.

"Honey, are you all right?" As an afterthought he addressed me and Ginger. "Ladies. Are you okay?"

"Yes," Honey said, "we didn't go in. We waited for the officers to arrive. They're in there checking it out." Honey opened her door.

"Stay here and I'll go see what's happening." Detective Montaine disappeared into the condo.

Time moved in slow motion until they came out. "It's all clear. It's okay for y'all to go in," he said. "But it's obvious someone tried to get in from the damage."

"Well, that's good because I'm about to pop." Honey laughed and the detective laughed with her like she'd just said the funniest thing ever. Boy, they had it bad.

"Skye, I need you to check and see if anything's missing," Detective Montaine said. He followed us back into the house and stopped to talk to the officers, one of them busy taking pictures of the doorframe.

I called Mitch and told him what happened.

"Honey, I'm almost home."

While the detective was downstairs talking with the officers, I dragged Honey upstairs where we could have some privacy. "I need to check on the map."

"I'd thought about that, too."

I checked behind the picture, hanging above our bed. Relief flooded through me when I discovered the map safe and sound. I released a sigh of relief. Had the intruder searched for the map? I didn't believe it was coincidence somebody broke into Mitch's store and our house. The treasure map was the connection.

"It's here, Honey. I've been thinking we need to tell Detective Montaine that I have a copy of the map." My legs shook like Jell-O, so I sat on the bed. All the energy drained from my body. Exhaustion overwhelmed me.

"I think you're right. This is getting too big for us." Honey sat down beside me, put her arm around my shoulder, and gave me a squeeze.

Staring at the floor, something white caught my eye. I picked it up. "Look, Honey, it's a business card from The Silver Spur. Did you pick one up the other night when we were there?" I flipped it over. A blank card stared back at me.

She reached and took the card from my hand. "No, I didn't. Did you?"

"No."

"Wow, this could be some kind of clue. Maybe the person who ransacked your condo lost it. Let's go show Robert what we found," Honey said.

We hurried downstairs and discovered Mitch talking to the detective. He came over and gave me a big hug. "Are you all right, babe? I was so worried."

"Yes, we're fine. We weren't home when it happened. When we got here I noticed the marks on the doorframe so we called the police and waited in the car. They cleared the place before we came in." I clutched his arm and squeezed it. I needed something solid to hang on to. "I'm sorry. I guess I forgot to set the alarm."

Mitch paced back and forth. "What do you make of this, Detective? First my store and now our home." Mitch punched his fist into his palm.

"Skye has a theory about the break-ins." Honey stood close to Ginger. They looked like they'd been rode hard and put up wet.

"Really," said Detective Montaine. "Do you care to share this theory with us?" His voice had an edge to it.

I cleared my throat, dry as the desert sand. "I wanted to tell you we kept a copy of the treasure map. We're wondering if the map doesn't tie in to the break-ins."

The detective removed his hat and ran a hand through his hair. "I'm not sure, but it's a possibility. Especially since someone tried to steal the original from you. If you want to keep the copy I'd put it in a safe."

I handed him the card. "I found this on the floor. Could it be a clue?"

He took the card and studied it. "The Silver Spur is a popular bar and a lot of people frequent it. Y'all need to be careful asking questions. Somebody thinks you're getting too close to them."

Mitch glared at me with steely eyes. "What's this about asking questions?"

I swallowed a lump in my throat. "I was going to tell you. The girls and I have asked some questions to the people who attended the party at Sylvia's, the night of her murder."

"Are you crazy, Skye?" Mitch looked at me like I was certifiable. "Are you trying to get yourself killed?"

# CHAPTER TWENTY-EIGHT

itch never raised his voice to me. "I'm sorry. It's just that Honey and I don't like being suspects. And now there's a possibility the map we found connects everything."

"Will you promise not to ask any more questions and let the detective do his job?" Mitch paced back and forth over our hand-looped rug.

"I'm sorry, Mitch, I can't promise I won't ask questions. But I'll promise to inform Detective Montaine of any new information we find. We've already learned a lot. Everybody seems to have had a motive to kill Sylvia." I steeled myself for another blow-up. It didn't come.

"You're a grown woman and I've trusted you all these years. I hope you'll change your mind, but if you don't, please take Honey and Ginger with you."

"I'm with your husband on this," said Detective Montaine. "I can't stop you short of arresting you and I'm not ready to do that. I have another person of interest, so you and Honey aren't first on the list anymore."

Ginger looked from me to Honey. "Isn't this wonderful? Y'all won't have to spend the rest of your life in the slammer. I shore was worried."

"We've kept you folks up long enough. We're going to go. Please call us if anything else happens during the night." The detective retrieved his hat and walked out with Honey.

"Ginger would y'all like to stay with us tonight. With everything going on I wouldn't mind having company and we can get an early start to Lake Lanier."

"Sure, if it's all right with Honey I'd love to." Honey agreed to stay so we could leave from here in the morning. I looked forward to filling my troubled mind with work. We said our goodnights and settled in for the night.

I snuggled up to Mitch, drawing energy from his presence. *Thank you Lord for our safety and for my wonderful husband...* I went to sleep before I finished my prayers.

Before I knew it, I rocked on the high seas in a schooner, dressed in a pirate's costume. Honey and Ginger were my shipmates. We wielded swords and an eye patch. A sloop closed in fast and I barked orders for everyone to ready their battle stations. The sloop came up beside us. The hearty buccaneers threw an anchor on our deck catching the railing. Hundreds of angry pirates boarded our ship. Among the pirates were: John and Stephanie Abbot, Raphael Hadley, Will and Joan Newton, Madeline Palmer, and Bernadette Jackson. Sylvia Landmark brought up the rear yelling, "Find my killer, find my killer."

Detective Montaine swooped in and grabbed Honey. "I'm kidnapping you!" Instead of Honey being scared she smiled and threw her hair over her shoulder. "I'm going with him Skye, guard our booty." Ginger unsheathed her sword and brandished it toward the advancing group of pirates. I hated to desert my post, but I needed to check on the map. I hurried below deck to search. It remained hidden under the desk drawer.

On my journey back to the deck, I ran headlong into the pirates rushing down the stairs. I planted my feet, raised my sword, and yelled, "You won't get away with this. We'll hunt you down." They began chanting, "give us the map, give us the map!" and rushed toward me. Will Newton grabbed my shoulders and shook me.

"Skye, Skye, wake up, it's me." I startled awake when Mitch shook me. "You were having a bad dream."

"Oh, Mitch, I'm so relieved. I dreamed I was a pirate and Honey and

Ginger were, too. Our ship was stormed by a band of renegade pirates and they demanded the map." I shivered and hugged him.

"Well, it was just a dream and it's over. Is there anything I can get you?"

"No, thanks. I'll try to go back to sleep." I told him I loved him and kissed him soundly. I tried to sleep, but rest didn't come for a long time. It seemed I'd just dozed off when my alarm sounded. I checked my phone and discovered I'd slept until eight. I needed to get up, fix breakfast, and get the girls up. We had another long day ahead of us.

I donned a pair of white capris and matched it with a yellow button-up shirt. I slipped on a pair of Keds instead of my usual flip-flops. I'd need the extra support while working. I knocked on the girl's door and informed them breakfast was cooking. I wrangled up something quick and easy – pancakes.

I'd just finished when Honey and Ginger dragged in. "Umm, it smells yummy."

"Look, Honey, a whole plate of 'em."

Honey grabbed the plate. "Okay, I have mine. You'll have to fix y'all some," she said. I wouldn't put it past her to eat the whole stack – and not gain an ounce. "Just kidding. I am hungry though."

We sat down and bowed our heads as Honey said a little prayer. I stabbed a couple pancakes before Honey took her share. Ginger poured a lake of syrup on her plate. We wolfed down the sugary treat in silence. I think we were all a little weary of our grim situation.

We tidied up the kitchen and headed to Lake Lanier. It took us almost an hour to get there due to morning traffic. I grabbed my tools and headed into Randall's cottage. While preforming a 360, I imagined all the changes I could make. The cottage already held charm, but I knew I could make improvements.

I strolled from room to room writing down measurements and changes I had in mind. "I'm going to work in the bedroom. Why don't y'all finish up in the living room?" I noticed right away how feminine the master bedroom looked. I'd like to make it more gender-neutral.

Something both sexes could enjoy. I laid my clipboard on the nightstand so I could use the measuring tape.

When I retrieved the clipboard, something familiar caught my eye. I picked up the little white rectangle with black writing. My breath caught. *Another business card from The Silver Spur.* What did this mean? A lot of people frequented the bar, but this pointed towards too much of a coincidence.

I called out to Honey and Ginger. They ran into the room to check out the commotion. "Look what I found! It's a business card from The Silver Spur." The girls' eyes widened.

"Wow! Do you think he's the one who broke in last night?" Honey took the card and turned it over. "It has a time and date on it!"

I grabbed it back. "That's tonight at 7:00. Do you think he's meeting somebody at the bar?"

"That's a possibility," Honey said. "Why don't we go undercover again? We could wait around and see who he meets."

"What if he sees us?" He'd probably recognize us.

"Well, we'll just tell him we're having a girl's night out on the town. Come on, we can do this," Honey said.

"I'm not comfortable in here anymore. How about we get out of here and question another suspect?" I had a bad feeling about this. I didn't want Randall to come home and find us snooping around. Even if we did have a legitimate excuse, we were invading privacy.

"Should we take this?" Honey flicked the card nervously.

"Yeah, let's take it so we can show Detective Montaine. But let's wait until we see if he meets somebody tonight." The desire to see who Randall met outweighed my fear. Did he want the treasure map, too?

I'd just cranked up the car when my phone played a familiar tune. "Hello."

"Is this Skye?" I didn't recognize the voice.

"Yes, who is this?"

"This is Bernadette Jackson. You were at my apartment the other day?" Fear laced her words.

"Yes, I remember. Is something wrong, Bernadette?" *Duh, of course something's wrong or she wouldn't sound like the boogie man was after her.* Honey tapped me on the shoulder and raised her eyebrows. I shrugged my shoulders.

A sob shot through the phone. "Oh, Skye, I've been arrested for Sylvia's murder. They have released me on bail."

# CHAPTER TWENTY-NINE

"What are the charges?" I mouthed "arrested" and pointed to the phone.

Silence filled the air. I waited on Bernadette to regain her composure. "Detective Montaine arrested me for Sylvia's murder. I would never hurt Sylvia. Yes, she was a witch at times, but like I said, I would always be loyal to her because of the help she offered me."

"I'm so sorry, Bernadette, but why are you calling me?" I shrugged at Honey and Ginger who were glued to my every word.

"I want you to help me. You have already been working to find the real killer, can't you continue? I did not do it, Skye. I need your help to get me out of this mess." She'd thrown a lot of information at me.

"Did the detective give you a motive?"

She explained between hiccups. "I was the last one to see her alive. I worked late the night of the party. Sylvia had a long list of errands she wanted me to run the next day so we were going over them. And that snooty old Abigail Smith told the detective that we'd argued earlier that day. Shoot, we argued all the time. She was obstinate and I have a temper. The combination equaled a recipe for disagreements, but we always worked them out."

"Abigail was Sylvia's cook, right?" She confirmed this. "Was there anything different about this argument that would cause Abigail to tell the detective?"

"Well, it's not what I said. It's what Sylvia said. I asked her for a month off to go see about my mother. She is not well and needed me at home. Sylvia had come to depend on me and when I asked for the time off she said 'over my dead body.' Who would have thought she would end up dead that night?"

"I see how that could look bad for you. Let me talk to Honey and Ginger and see what they say. If they're willing to help I'll see what we can do. That's all I can offer."

"I will take any help you are willing to give me. I must go now. Thank you." The phone went dead.

My hand shook. Honey and Ginger chomped at the bit to find out what Bernadette wanted. I hurried to get out of Randall's driveway. "Let's go get a Coke and I'll tell you all about the phone call." We headed over to the Tiki Hut for drinks and snacks. My stomach churned like an old timey washing machine. What had we gotten ourselves into?

"Spill it, Skye. Tell us about the phone call." Honey took a long drink of her Coke. At 80 degrees already and the humidity thick as pea soup, I anticipated a scorcher.

I wiped at the sweat running down my brow. "It was Bernadette. She's out on bail for Sylvia's murder."

"What! Why?" The girls asked.

I held up a hand palm out. "She was the last one to see Sylvia alive. The cook, Abigail Smith, told the detective they argued and she heard Sylvia tell Bernadette she could have some time off over her dead body. Unfortunately, she was murdered that night. She wants us to help her." I took my cold glass and wiped it against my forehead.

The girls looked at each other. "What do you think, Skye?"

"My gut tells me she didn't do it. Why would she bite the hand that fed her? I'm game if y'all are," I said.

"Count me in," Ginger said.

"Me, too." Honey signaled for a refill. "The first thing we need to do is talk to Abigail Smith."

"I agree with that." The Smiths lived on the premises of Sylvia's land. "Come on, girls. Let's hit the road."

The Smith's owned a small cottage, beautifully landscaped. A wooden fence enclosed a wildflower garden, and an abundance of colors painted the area like a portrait. I figured one of the Smiths loved to garden. A car sat in the driveway, I hoped an indication they were home.

We traipsed to the door and Honey used the decorative knocker to alert our presence. An older gentleman opened the door. An enormous smile illuminated his face. "Well, to what do I owe the honor of your visit? It's not often we have three lovely ladies come to our home." I explained our identity and that we'd like to talk to him for a few minutes.

He stepped aside. "I'll get my wife. I'm sure she'd like to see you." I seriously doubted she'd want to see us.

A gray-haired lady, back straighter than a soldier at attention, entered the room. "Hello." She had styled her hair in a severe bun at the nape of her neck. I recalled seeing her at Sylvia's while I worked. "You're that decorator aren't you?"

"My name's Skye." I introduced the girls. "We'd like to ask you a few questions about Bernadette Jackson." Might as well get straight to the point.

"She's right where she deserves to be." She crossed her arms and wore a satisfied grin. "I heard her and Ms. Landmark arguing the day of her murder."

Her husband's smile disappeared. "Now, honey. We're not sure she murdered Ms. Landmark. You know they argued all the time. It didn't mean anything."

"Don't honey me. I never did like her anyway, she talks funny."

"Well, I'm not so sure she did anything wrong. I like her."

Abigail placed her hands on her hips. She'd probably read Raymond the riot act when we left. We stayed a few more minutes, but didn't learn much more than we already knew – Abigail had it in for Bernadette, for a reason she only knew.

We sat in the car and discussed our next move. We had the rest of the day before we went to The Silver Spur. "Honey, do you have the list with you?"

"Yep." She pulled the list from her purse. "We've marked off everyone but Elizabeth Herring and Gloria Habersham two of Sylvia's bridge partners. Oh yeah, there's Amber Styles."

"How about we call Gloria and Elizabeth and see if they want to meet us for lunch somewhere?"

"I could go for some lunch," Ginger said.

"Good idea, Skye." Honey pulled out her phone to find Gloria and Elizabeth's numbers. Both of them agreed to meet us at Mary Mac's Tea Room. Having met them at the party, I recognized them right away. They waved us over to their table.

"Hi, ladies, thank you for meeting us," I said.

"Are you kidding," Gloria said, "I wouldn't miss going out to eat for anything. I'm just sorry it has to do with Sylvia's death. Bless her heart."

"Yeah, bless her heart." Elizabeth picked up her menu.

Honey and I swapped looks. She wasn't too upset about Sylvia's death. We marked our cards and gave them to our waitress, Beatrice.

"Well, you want to ask some questions while we're waiting." Gloria took a sip of her iced tea. "Yum, this is good."

"Could y'all tell me about Sylvia? And if anyone had a motive to murder her?"

Elizabeth laughed. "It'd be easier to tell you who *didn't* have a motive for murder? Sylvia rubbed everyone the wrong way like a porcupine at a bikini contest."

Ginger asked the obvious. "Why did y'all hang out with her if you didn't like her?"

I leaned forward, curious how they'd answer, but they just exchanged uncomfortable glances.

# CHAPTER THIRTY

Gloria wiped her mouth and laid her napkin in her lap. "She wasn't always like this. I've heard when her husband was alive she was quite normal. She changed after he died. She became hard to get along with and began acting eccentric. Like building that teahouse in her front yard."

"We've been bridge partners so long we felt obligated to stick it out. Of course, we were worried about Sylvia, but I never thought she'd wind up," Elizabeth paused a beat, "murdered."

"I'm surprised she didn't give you a hard time about the work you did for her. She probably would have, given enough time. She never left that poor Amber Styles alone. From the time she finished, until she hired you, she continually harassed her. She whined the job was a disaster and demanded her money back," Gloria said. "If I was that girl, I would've clocked Sylvia a long time ago." Our investigation proved there were plenty of people with motive. We just had to find the right one. I knew we were getting close, but we weren't there yet.

Everyone chose bread pudding with wine sauce for dessert. We sat a while, sipping coffee and talking, with these pleasant women. I couldn't imagine them being friends with Sylvia. But wasn't that what friends did? Stick with you through thick and thin? I hoped Honey would stick by my side if I needed her.

We voted unanimously to go by Amber's next, she was the last suspect on our list. Being our competition for several years, we knew where she worked. We arrived within twenty minutes.

A bell tinkled over the door. A disembodied voice from the back yelled, "I'll be out in a minute." Amber waltzed into the front room. She did a double-take when she saw us. "What are y'all doing here?"

"We'd like to talk to you about Sylvia's murder," I said. "Did you hear Bernadette Jackson's the main suspect? We're trying to help her."

"Why would you do that? She could be guilty." Amber placed a book of swatches down on the nearest table.

"I don't think she is. I wanted to ask if you knew who else might have killed her."

Amber placed her hands on her hips. "What you mean is did I do it. Not that's it's any of your business, but the answer is no. Just because she made my life a living nightmare doesn't mean I killed her. That old biddy tried her best to drive me crazy. She'd call me day after day demanding her money back, and she called some of my clients and bad-mouthed me. Most of them ignored her ranting, but I lost a few of them. I can't say I'm sorry she's gone. It's sure made my life easier." She sat down and leaned her arm on the table.

"Don't hold anything back on our account," Ginger said. Honey and I looked at her. She shrugged her shoulders.

We didn't stay long. I'd discovered what I'd come for. We had plenty of fodder to tell Detective Montaine. I doubted she'd spilled her guts to him like she just did. We said our good-byes and when she shut the door I heard the lock click behind us.

"I think I'll take a nap before we go out tonight. You're welcome to stay if you want."

"We need to go home and change. Remember, we're going undercover so we'll need our cowgirl outfits," Honey said. "And I'll need to check on Sam."

"Oh, this is going to be so much fun. I never thought I'd be a detective. I feel just like Nancy Drew." Ginger did a happy dance next to the car.

We managed to get back to the condo in short order. The girls went in with me to check it out considering the events of the past few days. I locked the door after they left, and set the alarm. I opted for a cool, afternoon shower. Refreshed I crawled between the covers. I went to sleep as soon as my head hit the pillow. When I woke, I called Mitch and told him the girls and I were going out. Bless his heart; he told me to have a good time. I just couldn't tell him what we'd planned and worry him needlessly. I donned black jeans paired with a dark blue shirt and slipped on my pant boots. The girls arrived around six thirty.

"Hey, Skye, I brought you a present." Honey handed me a large box wrapped with pretty ribbon. I excitedly shook the package.

"What? It's not my birthday." I pulled off the ribbon and tore the paper to reveal a shoebox. "Boots?" Inside, I discovered a pair of tan and blue cowgirl boots. "Oh, they're beautiful! Thanks Honey!" I took off my black boots and pulled on my fancy new boots. Now I'd fit in. I stuck my foot out and admired them. They fit perfectly. "How'd you know my size?"

"Checked your closet while we were searching for bad guys," Honey said.

"Come on, y'all. We've got work to do," Ginger said. She grabbed me and Honey and pulled us toward the door.

"All right, here we go!" I handed Honey the keys. "Shotgun!"

"Let's ask for the same waitress. I think she'll help us. What was her name?" She started the car.

"It's Maggie," I said. I remembered how her face lit up when she smiled. I imagined she'd done a lot of hard living during her life.

"Drive faster," Ginger nudged Honey in the shoulder, "we've got to get there by seven."

Honey responded like a NASCAR driver again; she sped up and wove in and out of cars. I held onto the handle above the door until we arrived in the parking lot. We hadn't even gone in yet, and my nerves were shot.

I remembered the smoke and the noise – nothing had changed. I gazed through the haze hoping to spot Randall, but I didn't see him. "I don't see him yet."

The hostess approached and asked if we wanted a table or a seat at the bar. We informed her we wanted to sit at one of Maggie's tables. She checked her clipboard, and sat us at a table. I didn't spot anybody I recognized, not that my friends usually frequented The Silver Spur.

Maggie came over and took our drink orders. We ordered sweet tea. I don't normally drink alcoholic beverages, but tonight might be the night to start. Maggie's eyes lit with recognition.

"Hey, y'all. You're the two ladies I waited on the other night. You must've had a good time since you're back so soon." She coughed a smoker's cough, and continued when she left to get our drinks.

We gathered in close and talked as low as possible. A daunting feat in a place yelling was the norm. "I don't see him yet," I said.

"What if he doesn't come? We could've been wrong and he wasn't gonna' meet anybody here." Ginger tore little pieces off her paper napkin and let them float to the table.

Honey glanced at the wall clock fashioned out of a lariat. "It's only five after. Give him a few more minutes."

"And I've got new boots to show off!" I said, shoving my feet around underneath the table in the unfamiliar, heavy boots.

Maggie carried our drinks on a tray. "Here ya' go ladies. Sarsaparillas all around." She smiled at us.

"These aren't Sarsaparillas," Ginger declared.

"I know," Maggie said, "but I just love saying that." She pointed to my feet. "New boots?"

I pulled up a pant leg so she could see it better. "Aren't they purty?"

"I'll be right back to take your order, I've got a pickup."

Ginger lifted her menu. "Let's hold these up so we can look around without raising suspicions." She took this detecting business seriously. I picked up my menu and began to study it when I saw, over the top, Randall Wade walking in to join a lone man at a nearby table.

# CHAPTER THIRTY-ONE

"That's him!"

"Where?" Honey and Ginger practically stood up looking around the room. I had the urge to clobber them.

"Shhh, we're trying to look disinterested. He's in the corner. I wonder who he's sitting with. Is it who he planned on meeting?" We had to figure a way to discover the identity of the mysterious man.

"How are we going to find out who he is?" Ginger attempted to squirt lemon in her tea, but the lemon popped out of her fingers and flew over to the next table. Oh-my-goodness! I buried my face in my hands so I couldn't see where it landed.

"Did one of y'all lose this?" Snake shoved the lemon in front of us. "Well, lookie here. If it ain't the pretty girls from the other night." Snake yelled to the next table, "Hey Tiny! It's our friends we met the other night." Not only did Tiny look, but everybody in The Silver Spur stared. Including Randall Wade and his companion. Randall looked me straight in the eye. So much for subtlety.

"Y'all want to join me and Tiny?" *Not on your life, bub.*

"Uh, no thanks, Snake. We're fixing to order something to eat." I glanced over at Tiny and he gave me a wave. *Lord please help us. We are going to need it tonight.*

"Okay. Just wave if you change your mind." Shoulders drooped he departed for his table.

"Well, Randall spotted us. We'll need to be real careful." I used my napkin to dab my forehead.

Maggie came over to take our orders. "All right, girls, what do y'all want?"

With all the commotion we'd forgotten about asking Maggie to help us. "Maggie, we need your help. See that man over there." She glanced at Randall's table. "No! Don't stare! Yeah, that's the one," I said. "We need you to find out the name of the man in the red shirt."

"And what they're talking about if you can," Honey said.

"Oh, I get it. Y'all are workin' for the government aren't ya'? Well, don't you worry one bit, ole' Maggie will help ya'. I'll swap tables with Lilly, that way I can spy on them." She clapped her hands together. "Oh, this is the most fun I've had in a long time." She pulled her pad from her pocket and took our orders. "I'll fill you in soon as I get a break." She winked and left through a haze of smoke.

I saw her go over and write down Randall's order. In a few minutes, she arrived laden down with our food. Nerves obviously hadn't affected our appetite. "Here ya' go." She handed out the food, leaned down and spoke in a low tone. "I know what that fellow's name is."

I leaned in close. "Really, how did you find out?"

"Why, I just asked him. Told him he looked like a fella' I went to school with. He said his name is Gill Brookhaven." She smiled wide as a country mile. "Did I do good?"

"You sure did, Maggie. Let us know if you hear what they're talking about." She left with a promise to keep us posted. "Hey, y'all know who Gill Brookhaven is?" They shook their heads. "He's the man that approached Mitch about the desk. He'd tracked the desk hoping to buy it. But after the break-in Mitch never mentioned him again. Now he meets up with Randall Wade. That is way too much of a quirk." My nerves vibrated with excitement. The puzzle pieces were coming together.

"I agree, Skye. They have to be in this together. I bet Randall broke into your house to search for the map," Honey said.

"It's beginning to make sense now. They've been after the map all along. What if they killed Sylvia while trying to steal the desk and John interrupted them?"

"Yeah." Ginger slapped a fist into her palm. "We've got 'em now."

"Detective Montaine's not going to believe us. He's convinced Bernadette is the killer. He never went along with the theory the map held value enough to kill for," I said.

"Okay, let's see what Maggie finds out. We need to keep eating so we don't draw attention." Honey took another bite of her steak.

"You mean any more attention," I said. We finished our meal and ordered dessert.

Maggie came over and sat down. "I'm on my break so I can sit a spell."

"Did you hear anything?" Honey practically bounced in her seat.

"Sure did. Them fellows was talking about birds. Something about a Martin."

We glanced at each other and said in unison, "Martinique."

She raised her eyebrows. "It's an island Maggie."

"Oh, well that makes more sense. They said something about leaving on a plane later tonight. What's all this about?"

I reached over and hugged Maggie. "We promise to fill you in later, but for now trust us, you're safer not knowing anything else."

She nodded, and patted the table. "This is the most exciting thing that's happened in here since Bobby Jack popped the question while Jimmy Sue was ridin' the mechanical bull." She left and I eyed the girls.

"Ladies, I believe we are in need of a vacation in the Caribbean on the island of Martinique."

# CHAPTER THIRTY-TWO

"Are you serious, Skye?"

"I am. We've got to clear our names and Bernadette's. At the same time we can search for the treasure. Then, maybe somebody will believe us." I glanced heavenward. *Lord please keep us safe and travel with us on this journey.*

"Oh, boy! I would have never believed giving up exotic dancing could be this exciting. I sure would've given it up a lot sooner." Ginger grabbed Honey's hands and squeezed. "Caribbean here we come!"

"They're leaving," I said, cutting my eyes toward the men who were approaching.

Randall stopped by our table. "Hello, Skye. Ladies."

"Hi Randall, we're just having a girls night out." I blurted it out as if we needed permission to have a night out.

"Well, you be real careful." He offered a salute and headed out.

"Boy, that was awkward," Honey said.

"Yeah, let's give them a few minutes to leave before we go. We need to make plans for tomorrow and I'll need to talk to Mitch."

"I'll check online and see if I can get tickets for tomorrow morning. I'll need to make arrangements for Sam while we're gone."

"I'll find out more information about Gill Brookhaven. I think Mitch mentioned something about him being a developer. I'll check the computer when I get home."

Mitch beat us home. I asked the girls in, but they wanted to go home and pack. I dreaded telling Mitch our plans, but I needed to get it over with.

I cleaned my face and put on my pajamas. Mitch sat in his recliner reading the latest issue of Art and Antiques magazine. I sat on the recliner's arm. "Mitch, the girls and I want to go to Martinique for a vacation and look for the treasure while we're there."

Mitch laid down the magazine and looked over his reading glasses. "You still think there's something to this map?"

"I do. The only way to find out is to see if it leads anywhere." I couldn't think of anything else to say. "Honey's making reservations for us to leave tomorrow."

"Since they've arrested Bernadette, I can quit worrying about y'all asking questions. I think it's a great idea for you to have a little fun."

*Wow, that was easier than I thought.* "Really? You're the best." I jumped up and gave Mitch a big sloppy kiss. "I guess I'd better pack." I ran upstairs and called Honey with the good news. She'd already booked our flight for 10:00 in the morning.

"Skye, I just know we're going to find the treasure. Have you researched Gill Brookhaven?"

"Not yet, but I'll do it before I go to bed. Leave your car here while we're gone and we'll take mine to the airport." Excitement coursed through my body like electricity. No way could I sleep. I took the opportunity to look up Brookhaven Development.

I shouldn't have been surprised to learn that Gill had a large tourist development in Martinique. The development consisted of condos, stores, hotels, golf courses, and restaurants. Were they traveling to Martinique for business? Or were they interested in the map, too?

I dozed off reading about Gill's projects. I startled awake when Mitch shook my shoulder. "Come on, honey. It's time to go to bed, especially if you're going to get up early in the morning." I saved the page in my favorites. I climbed in the bed and snuggled beside Mitch. I wouldn't see him for a while, and I wanted to remember that feeling.

I woke up when Mitch did. I had a lot to do, and I wanted to spend time with him before he left. Excitement kept me from eating much breakfast. Mitch and I discussed some of the attractions we might visit while on the island. Before I knew it, he had to leave. I clung to him as a shiver went through me. I didn't have a chance to worry much because Honey called and said they'd be on their way in a little while.

I'd just finished packing when the doorbell rang. Honey and Ginger waited eagerly for me to put my bags in the car. I helped them with their bags and we were on our way to a new adventure. Honey made our flights with Delta. I sat next to a young lady who told me about her best friend's destination wedding. Everyone chatted excitedly as the wheels touched down with a bump and a squeal. I couldn't believe how soon we'd arrived. Yesterday, we were in Georgia, and in a few minutes, we would exit the airport to a beautiful tropical island.

We hailed a taxi and gave him the name of the hotel that Honey had booked online. When we pulled up to a cluster of little huts, I figured the driver had misunderstood our directions. Honey showed him the information she'd printed off. He nodded and pointed to the shacks again.

"You've got to be kidding. This is the best you could come up with Honey?" I imagined sharing our quarters with all kinds of foreign critters.

"Well, it looked nice in the picture. They advertised it as unique," Honey said.

"I'd say it's *unique* all right."

"Let's go check the inside," Honey said.

The friendly manager, Bastian, offered to show us our hut.

"No bathroom?" I didn't see any doors except to a small closet.

"No ma'am. Communal bathrooms, one for the ladies, and one for the men."

I looked at Honey in disbelief. She just shrugged her shoulders.

"Just think of it as part of our adventure," Ginger said.

The manager smiled and offered a consolation. "We have Wi-Fi."

Hands on hips, I huffed. "Well that's good. I need to research Brookhaven Developments."

"You said Brookhaven Developments?" Bastian swatted at a mosquito using his arm as a blood bank.

"Yes, have you heard of them?" I realized that as a local, Bastian was a perfect source of information.

"I sure do. They are building the monstrosity on the north side of the island. It will bring many tourists. But it remained an untouched area for many years. After they build, it will be just like the rest of the island. It is sad." He shook his head. I asked for directions to Gill's project.

We changed clothes and opted for some fun since we'd spent all day traveling. Honey and Ginger talked me into para-sailing. Bastian recommended Coastal Parasailing. I'd never liked heights but everyone looked like they were having such fun flying high above the ocean. Anyway, they were securely strapped in. Nothing to it.

Before I had a chance to protest, the guide strapped me in. The ride started off fine. The boat accelerated slowly, and the girls waved and shouted their encouragement from the back of the boat. I waved back. I lifted higher and higher into the air. Suddenly, nothing but air filled the space under my dangling feet. I swayed from side to side. I glanced down and saw the passing ocean beneath me. Dizzy and sick to my stomach, I waved for them to stop the boat. They misunderstood. I wished I'd paid more attention to the hand signals they'd demonstrated in the safety briefing. Everyone waved back and the boat sped up. I tried to enjoy the beautiful sights, but everything passed in a blur. I said a quick prayer I wouldn't get sick in the air.

Finally, I began to descend. I stepped into the boat and everyone congratulated me and slapped me on the back. Then it happened.

# CHAPTER THIRTY-THREE

L ike an erupting volcano, everything I'd eaten that day came back up. The girls gave me room to hang over the side of the boat.

"Oh, Skye, is there anything we can do for you?" Honey rubbed my back, and handed me a towel. Ginger opened a bottled water.

"Honey, you can go next," Ginger said, looking at the rigging with newfound respect.

"That's all right, you go ahead of me," Honey offered.

Neither one of them took the challenge, so the boat captain took us back to the dock. I guess they decided they didn't want to have that much fun. It reminded me of the time Honey and I went to get our legs waxed. I went first and when I came out white as a ghost she decided she didn't want her legs waxed after all. *Some friend.*

"Let's get something to eat. I'm starved," Honey said.

"Me, too." Ginger rubbed her stomach.

Now that I'd emptied my stomach, I wanted to eat, too. We chose a seafood restaurant, The Blue Fin. We voted for grilled swordfish all around. While we waited for our food, we chatted about our plans for the next day.

"Let's turn in early tonight. I'd like to do some research on the computer and I'm too tired to go out on the town." I wanted to get an early start at the library.

"We need to hire a local to help us decipher the map," Honey said. "Let's do it tomorrow."

We hit the hay early and I awoke before the girls. I traipsed over to the communal shower and cleaned up. Anxious to get underway, I quickened my step. On the way back I ran into Bastian. I asked him the location of the library. He called a taxi for me. Tourists filled the town hurrying from one place to another. When I arrived, I told the librarian I'd like to research the Brookhaven Development and she gladly accommodated me. The locals weren't happy about the project that would destroy what little pristine property they had left on the island. Excited about my discovery, I hurried back to the hotel.

I had taken longer than I'd expected, and when I walked in, Honey ran up and hugged me. "Where have you been? We were so worried."

"I have some news to tell you, but I have to do a little more research before I'm sure," I said. "I've asked Bastian if he'd guide us while we're on the island. He knows a fellow that can help us decipher the map, who owns his own boat. He's familiar with every in and out of the island."

"Another boat?" Honey addressed me. "You sure you're up for that?"

"As long as I don't have to fly overhead, I'll be fine," I shooed them toward the showers so we could get moving.

Ginger and Honey dressed to blend in with the other tourists. Honey had on khaki walking shorts and a bright orange tee decorated with yellow flowers. She had put on a matching necklace and scarf around her neck. I looked at her feet.

"Honey, I think you'd better change those sandals to tennis shoes. We'll be doing a lot of walking."

"But they match my outfit." She wiggled her manicured toes. "Aren't they cute?"

"Yeah, they're cute, but they won't be so cute when your feet start hurting. Come on, we have lots to do. I told Bastian we'd meet him in front of the office."

Ginger had on orange shorts with a white tee. "Ginger, you'll need to wear tennis shoes, too."

Bastian waited on us. "Come on ladies, I will introduce you to Hosea. He owns the boat we will use." Bastian had commandeered an open Jeep for us to ride in. The breeze blew against my face. Still not used to my hair, I missed it whipping in the wind. The new style proved perfect for our open-air trip. I just finger brushed it when we stopped.

I appreciated the palm trees and the colorful exotic flowers as we made our way to the docks. We followed Bastian to what probably had been a beautiful boat at one time, but now I was afraid a stiff wind would come along and blow it apart. I couldn't say much for Hosea either. With scraggly hair and beard, and a face as craggy as the rocks on the side of a cliff, he looked ancient. We were going to put our lives in the hands of this man?

Bastian must have sensed my concern. "Do not worry about Hosea. He is very knowledgeable and will be able to take you where you want to go. Did you bring the map to show him?"

"Yes, but let's get on the boat first. I don't want anyone else to see." The girls and I made our way hesitantly onto the craft. It rocked from side to side. Oh, no! It reminded me of the motion from the para-sailing. I said a quick prayer I wouldn't get sick.

"Hey, you're not going to upchuck are you?" Ginger backed up a little and Honey followed suit.

I withdrew a little package from my bag and held it up for them to see. "I came prepared. I've already taken a Dramamine this morning in preparation for the boat trip. I see it was a good thing, too."

Honey and Ginger looked at each other. "Can we have one of those?" Honey grabbed for the package. We laughed and Bastian and Hosea joined in.

"Yes, that is wise," Hosea said.

We ducked our heads and entered the small cabin. I spread the map on an old table where Hosea studied it. "Yes. Yes. It is on the north side of the island. Let's begin our journey." We took a seat on a bench the length of the boat. I hung on for dear life as we picked up speed and jostled over the waves. We were thrilled when we saw a couple of dolphins playing and vied for a better view.

By the time we disembarked on the small secluded beach, we were a little green around the gills. A glistening waterfall flowed over the cliff. A breathtaking scene. God had certainly done some of his best work here.

Hosea pointed to the cliff. "Look! See the face on the cliff? The same one that is on the map."

"Wow, it sure is," Ginger said. "Look how there's stairs built in the side of the cliff."

"According to the map you must climb them to reach your destination."

"You're kidding, right?" I couldn't imagine climbing the steep rock on those precarious steps.

"If you want to follow the map you must climb them." Hosea pulled the boat up to the beach and we jumped off, anxious to reach our destination. Bastian ascended the steps first and Hosea brought up the rear. We made up the middle of the group.

By the time we reached the top, my legs were screaming. The girls sat on the ground rubbing their calves. As soon as I caught my breath, I discovered we weren't far from a strand of hotels in progress. Why did we just climb up a cliff we could have driven to?

"There's some buildings. Let's go investigate and see what we can find." Ginger stood and held on to the rock to steady herself.

Bastion confirmed my suspicion when he said, "This is the Brookhaven Development." We'd stepped right into Gill Brookhaven's territory.

"Look! There's the giant nose." Ginger pointed toward a large formation that resembled the drawing on the map. We were getting closer to the treasure. She ran over to the rock.

I held back and walked beside Hosea. "Where is the treasure located in relation to the rock?"

"According to the map, the treasure's close. I will need to study the layout a little more now that we are so close." When we reached the rock Hosea spread the map on the ground. We squatted around to follow his explanation of the area.

After measuring the map against the surroundings, he walked around the rock several times then paced off steps. He stopped and declared, "This is it!"

"Oh my gosh, let's start digging!" Ginger said.

"No, we can't dig," I cautioned. "Not in broad daylight. Let's come back tonight. Bastian, can you find something to mark the spot?" At least we wouldn't have to climb the cliff tonight since we'd discovered we could drive to the Brookhaven land.

"I will pile some stones over the spot so you can find it when you return. Do you want me to come with you?" I thanked Bastian for his offer to accompany us.

After descending the precarious stairway, we faced getting back into the rickety boat. I was thankful I'd brought Dramamine. When we arrived back on dock, my wobbly legs almost buckled. Honey and I supported each other as we waited for our sea legs to adjust.

"Let's go get a bite to eat and discuss our plans for tonight. We'll see if Bastian wants to go with us."

Bastian told us about a little out-of-the-way cantina with wonderful locally grown food. The cantina, designed like a hut, exhibited things from the sea. Fishing net covered one wall. Another wall displayed a colorful swordfish surrounded by starfish, the result created a wonderful ambiance. I ordered Caribbean jerk chicken with black beans and rice. Honey ordered pineapple black bean enchiladas and Ginger settled on crispy baked fish with curried sweet potato soup. We didn't accomplish much while we devoured every delicious bite. We had coconut-pineapple banana bread for an after dinner sweet.

"We'll wait until dark for Bastian to take us to the development." Bastian had already proved an asset to us. "We'll need shovels. Can you get some for us?"

"Yes, I can find some before tonight. Are you sure you want to do this? We could get caught."

"Nobody knows we're here. We'll be fine." I shouldn't have spoken so soon.

We went back to the hotel to get some rest before our adventure. I took the opportunity to call Mitch and tell him what a wonderful time we were having. I recounted my parasailing adventure and the boat ride to explore the coast, but left out the part about finding the location of the treasure, focusing on what a relaxing time we were having. I'd wait until we actually found it.

We slept the afternoon away and woke up late. We decided to eat light since we'd stuffed ourselves at lunch. The rest of the evening we spent sightseeing, exploring some of the local shops filled with hand-made souvenirs. When we'd returned to the hotel at dusk, Bastian had commandeered shovels and flashlights.

We hopped into the Jeep and wound our way through the bustling city. We'd all worn sneakers in anticipation of having to hike in. I wondered how far we'd have to park from the site.

Bastian parked near the row of hotels we'd seen from the cliff. The development was in phases of being finished. Each of us grabbed a shovel and walked toward the giant nose, being careful of the building equipment.

After an hour of digging, we were no closer. The ground, filled with gravel and stones, slowed our progress. A shovel tip broke off, and one of the flashlights failed, so we worked by the moonlight.

"Wait a minute, I have an idea," Ginger said. She grabbed a flashlight and ran toward the jeep. In a few minutes, flickering headlights headed our way.

"What in the world?" As the lights neared, I could see a Bobcat bull-dozer. "Someone's seen us!"

# CHAPTER THIRTY-FOUR

"It's Ginger!"

Sitting in the driver's seat, she grinned from ear to ear. She killed the motor and jumped down. "Surprised you didn't I?"

Surprised was an understatement. "How did you learn to drive a bulldozer?" Honey's big, round eyes reminded me of an owls.

"My step-daddy managed an equipment rental company and I learned how to drive some of the rigs on the lot."

All this time, I thought she'd gone into exotic dancing because she didn't possess any skills. Once again, I'd made an assumption before I knew the facts. I really couldn't wait to learn more about Ginger.

"Everybody move out of the way. Here I come." She hopped back on the Bobcat and started the engine. Bastian stood over the spot until Ginger saw where to dig. She'd scoop a little, then we'd check for the treasure. Whenever the blade bumped into something hard we'd gather around and dig with the hand shovels to reveal stones of various sizes. We were just about to give up when we hit the jackpot. Bastian's shovel struck something that gave way a little.

"Ginger, maneuver the 'cat so the lights shine into the hole." I shone my light into the pit where Bastian stood knee deep.

She maneuvered the rig so the lights were at an angle.

"It's the treasure chest!" Honey squealed. "Let's open it!"

It took him a few minutes of digging around the edges, but it finally broke free. Bastian used a crowbar to pry open the rusted lock. He opened the chest and we all gasped.

"Would you look at that loot?" Ginger said. We vied for the best position to see the treasure.

Honey ran her hands through the gems. "Can you believe this?" She held up a handful of gold doubloons and let them slide through her fingers.

"We found the treasure, we found the treasure!" Ginger danced around. Honey and I hugged each other and Bastian watched us like we'd all gone crazy.

"How are we going to get the chest out of the hole and carry it back to the Jeep?"

A stranger's voice called from the darkness. "We'll take care of that for you. Step away from the hole. Put your hands up and don't move." Out of the night, several men descended upon us. They bound our hands with zip ties and dragged us to a waiting van. Two men brandishing pistols demanded we get in back, where they blindfolded us. We could hear them arguing while getting the treasure out of the ground. Honey whimpered. One of the men knocked Bastian unconscious and I said a quick prayer for his safety. No buried treasure warranted losing our new friend.

After a few minutes, the engine started and we jostled in the back of the van as it lurched into movement. I couldn't really tell how far we'd gone, because the van twisted around unfamiliar roads. When we bounced over a particularly rough place, the driver slowed and honked the horn. I heard the grinding of an automatic door. We moved a few more feet and stopped. The back doors were jerked open and we were pulled out. Someone pulled my blindfold off and shoved me in a chair. I saw Honey, Ginger, and Bastian already seated. Bastian looked dazed and confused. *Thank you Lord we're all safe.*

"Well, well, who do we have here?" I recognized him as the man who'd met Randall Wade at The Silver Spur.

"You're Gill Brookhaven."

"That's right. And you're the infamous Skye Southerland." He shot Honey and Ginger a smirk. "These must be your friends Honey Truelove and Ginger Walker. And you are…?"

"My name is Bastian."

"He's not anyone you need to worry about, just our driver," I didn't want anyone getting hurt. I needed to keep them talking so I could buy us time. "Where is your partner?"

A man walked around the corner of the van. "You mean me?" I didn't like the sinister grin Randall Wade wore.

"Yes. I mean you." I'd had a hunch, but when I went to the library this morning I'd confirmed it. Gill and Randall owned Brookhaven Development together. "How did y'all find out we'd be here?"

Gill laughed. "Oh, it wasn't too hard to convince Hosea to help us." He slammed a fist into his palm. "We had people following you back in the states. We knew when you landed on the island and where you stayed. So when we found out you went off with Hosea we convinced him to share information with us. All we had to do was wait and let you lead us to the treasure. Now, it's all ours."

"You won't get away with this. Randall, we found the business card you left when you broke into the condo. And we found one in your cottage. We gave them to Detective Montaine. He'll be on your trail, like a dog on a bone, if we go missing."

"Yeah," Ginger said.

Gill eyed Ginger. "Hey pretty lady that was some fancy maneuvering with that Bobcat. I appreciate you finding the treasure for us. I've searched a long time."

"You broke into my husband's store didn't you?"

"I got one of my men to do it, but it didn't do me a bit of good. I still didn't have the map."

"So you tried to steal it from us?" Honey pulled at the ties that held her hands.

"That was one of my men. I don't like to do the dirty work."

I thought I had it figured out. Gill had hired a thug to kill Samuel

Baker and steal the map. Instead, all they found were the plans. "They killed Samuel for nothing didn't they? You didn't get the map, so Randall broke into our condo. When he couldn't find it you had somebody tail us. But why kill Sylvia? She presented no threat to you." How could anyone be so evil?

"Hey, I don't mind taking credit where it's due, but I didn't kill that old lady." He waved his gun around as he paced back and forth.

"Yeah, and I didn't break in your condo. I'm with Gill. I'm not about to get my hands dirty."

"What about the card we found in my condo and the one in your house?"

"Those were obviously planted by someone trying to frame me, don't you see? A lot of people go to The Silver Spur. Is that how you found out about our meeting there the other night?" Nobody answered.

Bastian had roused enough to speak and demanded an answer about his friend. "What did you do with Hosea?"

"You don't have to worry about him. He should be fine in a few days. He was very helpful." Gill and his goons laughed.

One of Gill's men shot us a look of contempt. "Boss, what do you want us to do with them? They'd make good fish bait."

"Yeah, but it's got to look like an accident. Put them on that excuse of a boat and blow it up. Nobody will be surprised."

Randall walked over and pointed his gun at us. "The sooner we get rid of them the better."

Randall's minions blindfolded us again and forced us back into the van. I heard the garage door raising and waited for the van door to slam shut. Instead I heard, "Don't make a move! This is the police and we have you covered. Put your hands in the air."

# CHAPTER THIRTY-FIVE

Somebody cut the ties binding my hands. "Here ma'am let me help you out of the van." An officer supported me while I slid out and stepped down. Honey, Ginger, and Bastian came next. A sea of cops filled the warehouse and surrounded Gill, Randall, and their men.

A man, exuding authority, parted the sea of officers. "I'm Inspector Kaan."

"How did you find us?" I didn't really care; I was just thankful they did.

"One of our locals found Hosea and took him to the hospital. He told us you were in danger. I imagine these hoods thought they'd killed him. We'll have guards outside his door while he's hospitalized."

He stepped back while his men handcuffed Randall and Gill. We'd finally solved Sylvia's death. Honey and Ginger came over and we hugged. "Ladies, I'd like for you to come downtown so I can get your story. Hosea mentioned a treasure. You can ride with one of my men."

Silence prevailed on the ride. I contemplated how close I'd come to death. I wanted to meet my maker, but not under these circumstances.

A medic checked us over, and bandaged Bastian's head wound.

We waited a while before Inspector Kaan joined us. "Ladies, I hope you are better. I realize you've endured a harrowing experience." I held Honey's hand on one side and Ginger's on the other. Another officer took Bastian and questioned him separately.

"Please tell me why you came to our island and how you got your-selves into this mess." We began talking at the same time. "Excuse me, ladies, one at a time please. Ms. Southerland why don't you start first?"

I told him about Sylvia's murder, and touched on our attempt to get some answers. I explained about the map we found and how there'd been several attempts to steal it resulting in Samuel Baker's death. How Detective Montaine arrested Bernadette for Sylvia's murder and she'd asked us to help. We discovered Randall and Gill knew each other and were leaving for Martinique, and we decided to follow them and search for the treasure at the same time. I stopped for a minute to catch my breath.

I went on to tell him about our trip with Hosea and how we'd climbed the cliff to discover the treasure and then returned to search after dark. Then I explained how Gill and his men kidnapped us. I gave him Detective Montaine's contact information.

"That's quite a story. I'll inform him we've apprehended these men, and checking out your story. They have denied killing this Sylvia Landmark person. I hardly think it will make much difference for them. With their list of other crimes they will not see daylight for a long time."

He questioned us for another hour or so and told us we were free to go as long as we promised to stay on the island until further notice. By the time we arrived back to the hotel, dawn had risen. I called Mitch and told him what happened.

"Babe, I'm going to fly over there. I'll book the first flight out."

I protested, but secretly thought I couldn't wait to see him. "You don't have to. We'll be coming home as soon as Inspector Kaan says we're free to go. Please don't worry about me. Randall and Gill have been arrested." Tears of relief filled my eyes. "Finally, we can rest at ease."

"All right, but if you're not on a plane tomorrow I'll be on my way. Please take care and call me as soon as you find out about your flight."

We said our good-byes and I crashed, hoping for a few hours of sleep.

"Hey, Skye, wake up. Ginger and I are going out to eat. Do you want us to bring you something back?" It thought I'd just dozed off when Honey woke me. But my phone said different.

I didn't want to stay alone. "No. Give me a few minutes and I'll get dressed and go with you." I pulled on a clean skirt, tee, and flip-flops and grabbed a hat I'd bought on our shopping trip. I'd fit right in with all the other tourists. "Where're we going?"

"Let's just walk until we find a restaurant we like," Ginger said.

"That's a great idea. I could use the fresh air and the exercise." I held Ginger's hand. "Ginger I want to tell you and Honey how sorry I am that I got you mixed up in this mess. I never dreamed we'd be held at gunpoint, witness a man murdered, and be kidnapped."

I'd grown to appreciate Ginger as a person and a daughter of God. We've all sinned and fallen short of the mark, but if God can forgive and provide us with a chance for a new life, who am I to begrudge Ginger a new beginning?

"I have to admit, I've never been so scared." She laughed nervously. "But I've never had such an adventure either. I just hope hanging around you girls isn't this much fun all the time."

We stopped at a crowded cantina. After we ordered fajitas, we went into de-stress mode. We talked about everything that had happened and the relief our nightmare had ended. After the delicious lunch, we walked around, finally able to enjoy the beautiful island without worrying about our fate. Everything looked clearer, brighter, almost as if seeing things in 3-D.

Later in the afternoon Inspector Kaan sent an officer to bring us to his office. He had good news and bad news. The good news – they found the treasure the kidnappers had tried to hide while they decided what to do with us. The bad news – they'd confiscated it for their government. We'd done something wonderful though – discovered a hidden treasure map and found the bounty. Easy come, easy go, as they say.

Inspector Kaan gave us permission to leave the island and I couldn't make reservations fast enough. We'd leave early the next morning. I called Mitch and gave him our flight plans. I longed for his arms around me. We found Bastian and told him how much we appreciated his help. He'd been to visit Hosea at the hospital where he recovered from his injuries.

# CHAPTER THIRTY-SIX

Thankfully, we experienced an uneventful flight. Mitch met us at the airport, and I hugged him like I'd been gone a month. "It's so good to be home!"

"It's good to have you home." He kissed me soundly. "Come on ladies." He grabbed my carry-on bag. "Your chariot awaits." Ginger and Honey trotted along behind us, tugging their rolling cases bulging with souvenirs.

We were in the car when Mitch dropped a bomb. "Skye, I hate to tell you this, but your shop's been broken into."

*Not again.* "What? When?"

"We're not sure when it happened. And we weren't able to tell if anything's missing. When you get home and rested do you want to go down and take an inventory? Detective Montaine wants to meet us. By the way, with the arrest of Gill Brookhaven and Randall Wade, they've released Bernadette."

"Oh, that's good news. I didn't think she had anything to do with it."

Honey and Ginger didn't even come. They were ready to go home. I saw a glimpse of red as Honey's Crossfire scooted down the road. I rested during the afternoon while Mitch worked from home.

"You ready to go to the shop, babe?"

"I guess I can't put it off forever. I'm anxious to see if anything's missing." We chatted while we drove. My heart broke when I saw my front window boarded up. "Mitch, why are we having all these robberies? Gill admitted to breaking into your store, but Randall said he didn't break into the house," I shook my head, "it just doesn't make sense. There's not much point to it now."

"Could be totally unrelated," Mitch said. "Let's leave this one up to the police, shall we?" He gave me a reassuring wink, and I agreed only too happily.

Detective Montaine pulled up about the same time we did. "Hello, Skye. It's good to see you back. How are Honey and Ginger doing?" So *now* we were on a first name basis.

"They're doing fine. I'm sure they'll be sorry they missed you." He smiled a crooked little grin. "I was glad to hear of Bernadette's release," I said.

He nodded, sober again. "Even without the missing Civil War sword, we didn't have enough to hold her."

"What Civil War sword?" Mitch loved Civil War history and possessed a great deal of knowledge on weapons from that period.

"We haven't released this information to the public, but we believe the weapon used to stab Sylvia was from a collection of Civil War swords. We discovered one missing from her home. We still haven't recovered it, but we haven't processed Brookhaven and Wade's homes yet."

"That's definitely new information," Mitch said.

"Okay, let's see if anything's missing." The detective gestured toward the door.

I unlocked the door and flipped on the light. I didn't notice anything out of place. It would take a while to check the inventory, and I'd need Honey's help for that. A sense of light-heartedness overcame me, until I entered my office. Papers were scattered everywhere, and my desk's drawers were pulled out and the contents thrown on the floor.

"Detective, it's going to take me a while to go through the contents of my desk to determine if anything's missing. Could I get back to you with the information?"

"That'll be fine. Just call me if you discover something." He shook hands with Mitch and they walked out together. My stomach churned and the hair on the back of my neck stood up. What did I have that someone wanted bad enough to break into my shop? Something the detective said resonated within me, but I couldn't worry about that now, I needed to focus.

Mitch came back in. "I sure am sorry." He swept his arm over the desk area. "You didn't need to come home to this. Can I help?"

"I think I'll call Honey and ask her to come down. She'll help me put this mess back in order." I called and she said she'd arrive in less than an hour. I encouraged Mitch to go back to work.

After Mitch left, I inspected the papers scattered on the floor. I tried to concentrate, but something Detective Montaine said still niggled at the back of my mind and I gave up working on my mess for the moment. I searched through the clutter on my desk and found a flash drive. I inserted it into the computer and waited for the pictures of Sylvia's house to load. I clicked on each picture, enlarging it until I came to the one I searched for.

I heard a noise and glanced up. "Oh, Will! I didn't hear you come in." I tried to keep my voice as steady as possible, but it shook anyway.

"I'm not here on a social call. I think you have something I want."

I palmed the flash drive before he could round the pile. I withdrew it from the computer and slipped it into my pocket.

"You've figured it out haven't you?" He glared at me.

"I think so. After I learned the weapon came from a Civil War collection, I remembered the sword I saw in your office the day we visited you. I thought it matched one I'd seen at Sylvia's, so I went through the pictures on the flash drive. I found one just like it. It's the same one isn't it?"

"Yeah." He pointed a gun at me. "And you *will* give me that flash drive."

My hunch proved right. He killed Sylvia. Gill and Randall told the truth; they didn't kill her. Wade had no intention of keeping me alive. I needed to keep him talking until Honey arrived. "Why would you kill your mother-in-law? She was hard to get along with, but surely not enough to kill. Was it the money?" I didn't realize how desperate he needed money and the length he'd go to get it.

The floodgates opened and the words flowed. "The old biddy. She thought she could jerk me around. One minute we'd be in her will, and if we so much as blinked she'd write us out. She wanted to control everybody including her own daughter."

Engrossed in his ranting, he didn't pay much attention to me. I reached over, pocketed my mini-tape recorder, and flipped it on. If I could get a confession on tape it could put him away for Sylvia's murder. I hoped I'd live long enough to hand it over to the police. I needed to keep him talking – although he didn't need much encouragement from me.

"Joan's daddy promised to leave the sword to me. He knew how much I wanted it for my Civil War collection. He didn't put it in his will, but Sylvia knew he meant for me to have it. She hung on to it like a flea on a dog and told me I'd get it over her dead body."

"I guess she was right." He laughed manically. "I thought Joan would get her inheritance and we'd just kill two birds with one stone. But no, she left the bulk of her inheritance to her hair stylist. Who in their right mind leaves their money to their hair stylist?"

I resisted checking the device. I didn't want him to suspect I had stuck the recorder in my pocket. My heart thumped so fast, I feared my heartbeat would cover his confession.

He laughed again. "Oh, that's right, she wasn't in her right mind. Crazy woman – building a tower in her front yard."

He paused and looked into space like he traveled to a place only he could see. Maybe, if I showed some compassion, he'd keep talking. I needed him to come right out and make a confession. I fought to sound sympathetic and caring. "She was downright mean. I've seen her in action. It's terrible she didn't give you the sword your father-in-law promised to you. And it was plain spiteful she left her money to Raphael." I paused a second for courage. "Is that why you killed her?"

"Sure I killed her. She got just what she deserved and I'm not sorry for it. Now hand over the flash drive and get away from that desk."

He indicated with his gun for me to move. I skirted around the desk and handed him the flash drive. I didn't have much of a choice with a gun pointed at me. I silently prayed he'd take it and leave me unharmed.

"Now all I need to do is get rid of—"

A crash from behind Will startled both of us. He turned to see what happened. I grabbed the lamp from my desk and hit him in the head. He fell like a freshly chopped tree. From behind an armoire, a familiar figure emerged.

Honey saw the body on the floor and raced over, almost knocking us both down in her rush to embrace me. "Oh, Skye, I'm so glad you're all right."

"We better make sure he's not going to cause any more trouble." I searched the room. "Hand me some of that drapery cord!"

"This is ninety bucks a yard!" She tossed it to me.

"Gives a new meaning to 'styles to die for,'" I quipped, winding the hand woven silk sash around his wrists and ankles. "There."

She dialed 911 while I tugged at the knot to make sure he couldn't get up if he came to before help arrived.

Cellphone to her ear, Honey told the dispatcher what happened.

"How did you know I needed help?"

"When I arrived, I noticed the door was slightly open. I knew you wouldn't leave it open when somebody had just broken into the shop. I tiptoed in behind the new shipment of samples and hid, listening to Will spill his guts. I tried to get closer so I could clock him, but I forgot about that pile of new sample books and tripped. That's when you clobbered him. Way to go!"

Ginger came in and examined the scene. "Wow, I missed all the excitement. I was in the car listening to my favorite song by Allen."

While we explained to her what happened, sirens wailed from a distance.

"I'll go out and tell them we have the suspect well in hand," Ginger said.

In a few moments, she led Detective Montaine in, followed by several uniformed officers. A deputy roused Will, took him into custody, and questioned me for a few minutes. I couldn't wait to give them the tape of Will's confession. The detective just shook his head when he discovered Will had killed his own mother-in-law.

As we locked up, I invited Honey and Ginger over for supper. We couldn't wait to give Mitch all the details of Will's arrest.

---

A month has passed and our lives have settled down. I'm happy to say, Ginger is doing well and she's still helping us at Stylish Décor until she can find a permanent position. Honey and I were cleared of any wrongdoing, and she's been dating Robert, as we call him now. They've really hit it off. I wouldn't be surprised if it developed into a long term love affair.

Mitch and I have cleared our calendars and leave in the morning for a much needed vacation. I can't wait to show him Martinique.

CPSIA information can be obtained
at www.ICGtesting.com
Printed in the USA
FFOW02n1016121115
18475FF